"You thought I was going to make love with you?" John demanded.

"Yes. No. I mean…" Wanda faltered.

"Glad I'm not the only one confused by this arrangement of yours."

He hovered over her. She hated when he did that. It never failed to make her feel petite, which for her translated to insignificant. She sprang to her feet.

"I'm not confused, and you can't say it wasn't on your mind," she said. "Sitting there giving me those bedroom eyes. You even took off your glasses to enhance the effect."

"I took off my glasses because I was chopping onions. So don't flatter yourself—I have no intention of seducing you. Not that it wouldn't be easy to do. You were panting and puffing louder than an overheated steam engine."

"Excuse me?"

"That's right. Making love to you is the last thing on my mind, but you must admit, when a man can't kiss his own wife without suffering backlash and being branded a seducer, something's very, very wrong. It's driving me crazy trying to read your mind." He stopped and took a breath, running a hand through his hair. "I'm going to go now and get a good night's sleep, and on Monday I'm going to show Jackson the new designs. You see, Wanda, I can only deal with one crazy at a time."

"And you prefer Jackson?"

"He's less complicated," John said, and went looking for his coat.

"Then maybe you should be wooing *him*," she retorted, but John was already out the door.

Dear Reader,

We have two exciting and very different stories for your enjoyment. Gwen Pemberton is a talented new author who won the Golden Heart Award for best short contemporary romance novel at the national 1996 Romance Writers of America conference. At the glamorous awards banquet—the Oscars of the romance world—an excited Gwen accepted her statuette and was able to announce that she had sold that book, her first novel, to Love & Laughter. We hope you will enjoy her winning entry, *Wooing Wanda,* as much as the judges did!

Charlotte Maclay, a favorite with readers of Harlequin American Romance, has written a delightful tale of opposites forced to share a hotel room in a convention-filled Chicago. It's the story of a heroine, a straitlaced lingerie designer, who's just dying to be *bad,* and a hero who's determined to keep his hands off! Fun and games ensue throughout *Accidental Roommates.*

So give yourself an evening off—you deserve it!— curl up with a good book and indulge yourself with Love & Laughter!

Humorously yours,

Malle Vallik

Malle Vallik
Associate Senior Editor

WOOING WANDA
Gwen Pemberton

Harlequin Books

TORONTO • NEW YORK • LONDON
AMSTERDAM • PARIS • SYDNEY • HAMBURG
STOCKHOLM • ATHENS • TOKYO • MILAN
MADRID • WARSAW • BUDAPEST • AUCKLAND

ISBN 0-373-44030-8

WOOING WANDA

Copyright © 1997 by Gwendolyn Pemberton

This edition published by arrangement with Harlequin Books S.A.

® and TM are trademarks of the publisher. Trademarks indicated with ® are registered in the United States Patent and Trademark Office, the Canadian Trade Marks Office and in other countries.

Printed in U.S.A.

A funny thing happened...

And where did you two meet?

I get this question often when people look at my calm introspective husband and then at me, Ms. Queen of Effervescence. From the looks on their faces, I guess they're wondering how two people so different could have been in the same place at the same time to have even met. Our answer is simple—we met at work—but I've also run across couples that have made me want to ask the same question.

That got me thinking. It's one thing to know you and your future spouse are opposites, but it's a differently tied knot if your soul mate does a one-hundred-and-eighty-degree turn *after* the "I do's" are said.

Imagine the maze of compromises and adjustments such a couple would have to navigate on their bumpy road to love.

Imagine the comedy of errors.

That's what I did, and that's how I came up with *Wooing Wanda.*

Have fun!

—Gwen Pemberton

To the guy I met at work, and special thanks to
Lynn Michaels and to my Tribe—
Sally, Elaine, Liz, Tracy, Linda and Jenny.

1

JOHN ROCKMAN GLANCED at his watch. Twenty minutes before midnight, and he was home already. Had he been speeding? Too bad the cops hadn't stopped him. He would have gladly paid a ticket to buy extra time for concocting a believable lie. It had to be a good lie, too. He'd been late every night for the past two months and Wanda was no longer buying the truth.

Rain pattered on the roof of his Honda hatchback. The wipers worked overtime, doing nothing to improve visibility, so he squinted through the waterfall and eased the car into his driveway. The headlights flashed onto the living room windows and reflected a harsh glare into his eyes. John slipped smoothly into a scene from an old B movie.

"I'm innocent...innocent I tell ya," he said in his best Hollywood-style voice.

"Come off it, Rocko. You're late again." He deepened his voice, and tossed the words out the side of his mouth.

"Yeah, but it ain't my fault. Blame Jackson, he's the one who wanted more changes in the design."

"That's what you said last time."

Right. Even he was having trouble believing it; why should Wanda?

He switched off the headlights, then the engine, and

sat in the dark, listening to the rain and thinking of an alibi. No use. Lying was not his forte; he was stuck with the truth.

What would Wanda say tonight? Not much of anything, he hoped, scanning the dark three-story house. She was probably asleep, swallowed in one of his shirts, with her wild, blond curls covering her face.

He pushed down his glasses and massaged the bridge of his nose between his eyes, trying to ease the pain spreading somewhere behind them.

A dull ache fanned out from his shoulders and traveled the length of his stiff spine. In seven weeks, he would turn thirty-five, too young to be aching in all these places. Maybe he had worked too late.

He looked out his side window, but saw nothing beyond the rain washing down its surface. His breath fogged the glass. The interior quickly grew dank, stuffy; he preferred the freshness of a downpour to this. With umbrella in hand, he stepped out of the car and right into a muddy puddle.

Water pooled around his ankles as he tried opening the umbrella. It stuck halfway. After a few violent shoves, he forced it open. A loud rip filled his ears. John looked up into the sky through a large hole.

"Oh, damn," he said. Tucking the broken thing under his arm, he rushed up the stone path to the safety of his front porch.

He stood fumbling in the darkness, searching for the keyhole, finally opened the door and stepped into the silent foyer. His hand swept the wall, feeling for the light switch; found it and flicked it a few times. Nothing.

He walked into the living area, the squeaking of his wet soles echoing through the room. He felt for the light switch. Again nothing. Power outage, or Wanda, he wondered? He would bet on the latter, but what did she do this time, unscrew the lightbulbs?

"Not funny, sweetheart," he said, setting his work on the floor and inching into the room.

Left foot, together…right foot, together, he two-stepped toward his target, the art deco lamp next to the chaise longue. His arms outstretched, he probed the air with his fingers. At last, he reached the spot where the chaise should have been. The space was empty.

Rearranging the furniture on me. She must be really pissed, he thought. A dozen roses, special delivery, should do the trick. That little florist next to his office always had a nice selection. He'd see to it in the morning.

He reached out again, walked a small circle, and stopped. This was hopeless, he concluded, searching his pockets for the matches he kept for clients who smoked.

"Can't get this old Scout, Wanda," he said, striking the head.

The match flared. John squinted, not believing his eyes. The small flame fizzled.

"What the…" A ribbon of smoke filled his nostrils with the stinging odor of sulfur.

No, this can't be! His eyes were tired and the light too dim. He quickly lit another match. This time his mouth fell open as the area around him brightened. The living room stood empty—not a chair, not a table, not a picture on the wall. And not a single lamp.

The flame burned down, singeing his skin—just as reality hit. John dropped the match, shook his hand and brought the injured finger up to his mouth. He stood a moment in the dark, then roared like a cave-man.

"Wanda!"

"YOU TOOK the lightbulbs?"

"Yep," Wanda answered her sister, Dusty.

"Every last one?"

"Even the bathroom night-light," Wanda said.

She burrowed into the soft purple cushions of Dusty's wicker couch, and moved the bright pink telephone from her stomach, where she'd been cuddling it, over to the coffee table. She drew her knees to her chest and covered them with her faded blue sweatshirt. Dusty sat across from her, on the edge of the yellow love seat, shaking her head the way only a big sister can.

"Toilet paper, shaving cream, his clothes?"

Wanda nodded as Dusty went down the list. "All packed and gone."

"Gone where? Did you put it in storage?"

"You could say that."

"Girl, you do some thorough housecleaning. I hope you left a note, at least."

"A card. It said, 'Happy Thirty-Fifth.'"

"Well, that must have explained all," Dusty said. "What were you trying to do, soften the blow?"

"In case I'm still here when his birthday rolls around, I didn't want him to think I'd forgotten."

"No, you thought of everything, from the mood lighting right down to the Hallmark card. But an empty house...that hardly qualifies as a proper present. Just imagine this scene—man comes home tired—"

"Late." Wanda pointed her finger.

"Okay. Late...and tired...very tired. He finds his house empty. Burgled, he presumes. His wife is missing. He panics...she's been kidnapped...."

"He'd think no such thing. That's much too dramatic for John. With him, everything is logical, clearcut and conservative. That's the problem." Wanda hugged her knees.

"No, the man comes home and finds his house deserted. That's the problem. What are you trying to do?"

"I'm trying to save him. I'm trying to get my real husband back."

"By leaving?"

Wanda jumped from the sofa, walked to the windows and gazed out. The morning sun shone in the glass panes of the neighboring building. Its reflection was like a seal, a promise of another warm, bright autumn day. Darn the weather for mocking her mood. She felt so chilled, so gloomy.

She walked back and flopped onto the sofa. "Granny always said, 'Drastic measures for drastic times,' and I've already tried everything I know," she said.

"Could talking have been one of those things?"

"He just pushes the Mute button. Click, off goes my sound and in walks Rocko. Either that, or he starts with the moves."

Dusty frowned and shook her head.

"The into-the-bedroom-moves," Wanda explained. "The next thing I know it's morning, and I can't even remember where we left off, conversation-wise—as if it matters. He's up and gone to the office before 5:00 A.M. Sneaky way to win an argument, wouldn't you agree? No, Dusty, I've got to do this before it's too late. He's become a workaholic...he's obsessed. I don't want him dropping dead at his retirement party like Dad.''

''John is nothing like Dad.''

''He's nothing like the man I married either. He's become so...rigid. It's destroying his work, and *that's* destroying him. His last projects, the office buildings...they looked like boxes. Everything he's doing looks that way, and will until John breaks out of his own box.''

''So what happens when he calls? Does this drama have a script, or is it straight improv?''

''I arrived here last night. If he hasn't called yet, he won't call until Sunday, his one day off.''

''I don't get it. He'd worry you may forget his birthday, yet he won't call to find out if you're here?''

''Where else would I be? He knows I hate hotels. That leaves you.'' Wanda tapped her temple. ''Logic, remember. No, he won't call.''

''I guess that's why you've been carrying the phone from room to room.''

Wanda looked at the telephone sitting in the center of the glass table. It was hot pink but cold silent. More than anything, she wanted it to ring, and for John to be on the other end. But she knew better. He'd get caught up in his work and not think of her until he started for home. Then, it would be too late; he wouldn't call and chance disturbing Dusty.

''There's more,'' Wanda said, lowering her head and peeking up at her sister. ''I want a baby.''

''Come again,'' Dusty said.

''Don't look at me like that.''

''Like how?''

''Like you'd better grab the net before I get away.

I'm not crazy, I'm old…and I want a baby before I'm too old.''

"I'm four years older than you. I'm not screaming about my biological clock."

"Maybe you would, if you were married."

"Ouch," Dusty said, exhaling slowly. "I'm not the one sitting in my sister's apartment after emptying my house and deserting my husband."

Wanda pushed the curls out of her eyes and looked straight at Dusty. "I'm sorry. That didn't come out right. I meant, you would understand if you'd been married for ten years, and all you heard was, 'Not now. Let's wait another year.' I'm tired of waiting. I want a baby, John's baby, and I want it now."

"Obviously you paid no attention in health class. There's this little matter of a nine-month holding pattern, and that other little matter of physical proximity. You'll run into a bit of trouble, with John in D.C. and you down here in Richmond."

"Yes, but I have a plan."

Dusty twisted her mouth and crossed her eyes. "Nope. I don't want to hear it," she said.

"Shut up and listen. It's a good plan—a bit wild…."

"What plan of yours isn't?"

"They always work," she countered. Dusty raised her brows, and Wanda reluctantly added, "Most of them work…after a few glitches."

"This one doesn't involve me? Please say it doesn't involve me."

"Just listen. You'll love it."

"I was afraid you'd say that," Dusty groaned as she leaned closer to her sister.

JOHN DROVE WITH his windows down, radio blasting, his eyes forced open, and his attention locked on the street that cut its way between the rows of maples. He rounded the driveway of R and S Architects, thankful he hadn't dozed off behind the wheel.

The night before, he'd fallen asleep sitting on the bedroom floor, his back against the wall. When he awoke, his joints unfolded painfully, and his legs refused his weight. He struggled to make sense of the empty space and the birthday card in his lap, but a haze clouded his brain.

Now, he climbed the back stairs to his office, still confused, but pleased with himself for keeping extra clothes and toiletries at work. He only hoped he could shave and brush his teeth before anyone saw him. Quickly, he opened the back door and immediately banged into his partner, Larry Shu.

"What's going on?" Larry asked, whipping his focus from John to the office and back; his long, dark hair slapped him in the cheeks each time.

"I don't know. Did she call here?" John asked, looking down into his partner's flushed face.

"She who?"

"Wanda."

"Wanda? No, why? Does she know anything about this?"

Just then two men, struggling with a heavy piece of furniture, made their way down the hall.

"Coming through," one of them shouted a bit late, and knocked Larry out onto the stoop.

John watched as the men passed the open doorway, then disappeared down the hall. They were carrying a dresser—his bedroom dresser.

"What's going on?" he asked, pushing past Larry.

"What's going—" Larry lifted his face skyward, shook his head and screamed. "Help!"

John stopped in the hall, his mouth open, his forehead creased with frown lines. He watched as two other men tried fitting a cream-colored chaise through the office door.

"That's my couch!" he said.

"Yes," Larry said, "and your tables, and your chairs. Your whole house, man. Why is your house coming to work?"

"When did this stuff arrive?"

"Seven o'clock…maybe earlier. When I got here, it was here. But who cares. Get it out."

John glanced out the front door. His refrigerator sat on the sidewalk and boxes littered the small yard. Inside, boxes cluttered the hallway and stairs as far up as he could see. He couldn't squeeze through the narrow path without bumping into a column of them. They tumbled in his wake. He heard Larry yelp, and turned to see him stumbling over the heap, trying to catch up. John didn't wait, but strode to the far corner.

He pushed the door of his private office, and when it didn't budge, he put his shoulder against it and shoved. The sound of furniture scraping against the floor sent a shiver up his spine, but the door opened just wide enough for him to slip inside.

"Oh, brother," he said, surveying the room.

His queen-size mattress, his night stand and a stool were wedged into the small space. Suitcases covered his desk. A large box sat on his drawing table. It was filled to the top with lightbulbs.

"Very poor design concept," Larry said, poking his head into the space and clucking his tongue. "And you… You look like yesterday's fried noodles."

John wobbled across the mattress, stopped by his desk and stared out the window. The movers were making their way up the sidewalk with the refrigerator.

He had seen enough. He squeezed past Larry, and entered the bathroom. He hung his suit coat on the door hook, stripped off his shirt, folded it and placed it on the counter. He plugged in an electric razor and swept it across his face. In his mirror, he could see Larry blocking the doorway, his eyebrows drawn together so tightly they almost touched. One of the movers hovered behind him.

"All done," the man said, holding a clipboard and writing as he talked. "It's all off the truck and off the lawn. So what're you folks doing, turning this place into a storage or something?"

"John? Are we?" Larry's voice climbed an octave, wavering somewhere between tenor and second soprano.

"Wanda left me," John said through a mouth full of toothpaste.

"What?"

"No, not for good, for effect. She making a point, or so she thinks, and as usual she's gone overboard. Quality time," he continued. "That's what she's harping on about. If you want the truth, she has too much free time. Me, I have schedules, deadlines, contrary clients. I have a long-range plan—that she bought into, by the way—but free time I don't have."

John rinsed his toothbrush, put it away and began wiping the sink and mirror with a paper towel.

"Of course I work long hours," he said. "I'm not the one who quit my job—she is. Because they won't let her work part-time from home, she calls them old-fashioned, antifamily and rigid and walks out. And according to her, I'm worse than they are.''

John folded and refolded the damp paper towel until it was a two-inch square.

''Rigid,'' he said, pointing the towel in Larry's face. ''Me, rigid.'' Then he dropped it into the wastebasket.

''Whoa, back up. What are you talking about?'' Larry asked.

''Wanda. Wanda and her quality-time craze. And that's not all. She's mad about the puppy, too.''

''Who could be mad about puppies?'' asked the mover. ''Puppies are cute.''

''And did I mention the baby?'' John continued. ''If I had to choose, I'd take the puppy. They're demanding and messy, but at least you avoid college tuition.''

''I like babies. They're cute, too,'' the mover said.

''Do you mind?'' Larry glared at the man, then turned back to John. ''What baby?''

''I like babies. How can she say I don't like babies? We're just not ready to have one.''

''Maybe you and Wanda should go on one of those talk shows,'' the mover said. ''Not that I don't like listening, but you'll get more suggestions from a larger audience, know what I mean?''

''Who *are* you?'' John asked.

''Danny, your friendly mover.''

''How about moving yourself out of this private conversation,'' John said.

''Sure, I'm finished here anyway, but I need you to sign here, here and here,'' Danny replied, flipping pages and handing the documents to Larry, who absently held them out to John.

"I came home to an empty house. The furniture was gone and so was she."

"Well, we know where the furniture is. Where's Wanda?" Larry asked.

"Her sister's, probably."

"What do you mean, probably? Haven't you called?"

"She took the phones."

"Phones?" said the mover. "You need phones? Check the blue box in the hallway, but look, I need a Hancock from one of you guys."

"You can take all this back, can't you?" asked John, while putting on a clean shirt that he'd pulled from his bathroom closet.

"Sure. You want to pay for two moves...no problem by me."

John took the flip chart from Larry, scribbled across the pages and gave it back to the man.

"Return to sender," he read. "Okay Elvis, you got it."

"My ninety-nine-year-old grandmother has a saying for this," Larry offered, after the mover left.

"What is it?"

"Don't know. She's full of old Chinese sayings. She'd definitely have one for this situation."

John groaned and walked out the back door. Larry followed as close as a shadow.

"Are you leaving?" Larry asked.

"Yep. I'm taking the day off."

"You never take days off. What about Jackson? He'll want to see your new designs on Monday."

"I'll have things back to normal long before then, but if he happens to call, tell him I'm away doing an on-site inspection, checking for structural damage."

"What site? Where are you going?"

"Straight to the epicenter herself," John said and climbed into his car.

"Don't go there angry," Larry shouted.

Not a chance. He would face this the way he'd face any problem, in a logical, rational manner.

"RING, YOU stubborn monster. Ring already."

Wanda held the phone close to her face and shook it a few times before returning it to the coffee table. "How's my plan going to work if you don't ring?"

She leaned back on the sofa and folded her arms across her abdomen. It was a good plan—even Dusty had to admit that. Actually, she'd said it was so farfetched, it probably would work.

Well, *she* didn't think it was all that far-fetched. And there was no probably about it. It was definitely going to work. Dusty had agreed to help; now all she needed was John to cooperate.

She looked at the phone and made a face. Here she was, fixing their marriage, and he was making even that difficult. And their marriage needed fixing. It was a long way from what she had envisioned it would be—a partnership, built on love, sharing, and open communication. She had memorized those words from an article she'd read in a women's magazine. Too bad John hadn't read the same article. He thought of their marriage as a logical solution to their longdistance courtship.

Well, she had reintroduced the long-distance element, and they would discuss the courtship aspect later. That was all part of her plan, but missing him wasn't.

Wanda closed her eyes and imagined him on the

sofa with her. She could almost feel his warm, solid body pressing against hers, could feel him nuzzle her shoulder with his slightly bent nose.

He'd broken it in a childhood accident. Now, when he laughed or smiled, it twisted to the right. She loved that nose. Just as she loved the way he tickled her neck with his full lips, and blew his warm breath into her ears.

She tingled from head to toe just thinking about it. She sprung to her feet.

Stop it, girl. If you can't control yourself now, what will you do when you see him in the flesh?

Flesh. She tingled again.

"Scratch that word from your vocabulary, honey," she said, shaking herself and marching into the kitchen.

She needed a distraction. That was the best way to keep her mind focused. She paced the small area, searching for one, and grinned when she finally found something to do. She took two place mats, two bowls and two spoons out of the cupboards, and began setting the table. She would have everything ready when Dusty returned from the corner store with the deep chocolate, double fudge ice cream. What better way to celebrate the launching of her plan?

Suddenly, the doorbell chimed. Just like Dusty to forget her keys, Wanda thought, already tasting the ice cream as she rushed down the hall.

"Hope you bought enough," she yelled, unlocking the dead bolt. She threw open the door and froze.

John filled the entrance, his brown eyes looking big and sad behind his glasses, his smile slow and tentative. He held flowers in one hand, a shopping bag in the other.

"A dozen roses and a bottle of champagne should cover it," he said, presenting his packages.

Wanda looked back at the phone sitting where she left it, and then looked up at John. He wasn't just making it difficult, he was wrecking her plan even before it got off the ground.

"You were supposed to call first," she said.

"I thought I'd show up in the flesh." His rich voice rolled out, deep as a jazzman's bass fiddle.

Was it her imagination, or did he intentionally drag out that last word? Before she could decide, he leaned down and kissed her forehead.

His warm, moist lips burned her skin. Everything in her center tightened, then released. Again, every nerve ending tingled. Those darn tingles. They'll be the death of the scheme, she thought.

"Oh, heck," she muttered, and did the only logical thing. She pushed him away, and slammed the door shut.

2

"WANDA! OPEN THE DOOR, honey. No more games. That little trick with the furniture was enough. We have to talk, now. Come on, Wanda...Wanda?"

No. She wasn't ready to talk. Not yet, and certainly not in person. What she had to tell him was best done over the phone, but John had ruined that option. She stood with her back against the door, holding her breath and wishing she had foreseen this. Of all the times he could have chosen to become spontaneous, he had chosen this moment.

Wanda smiled. Actually, things were going well, even if they were happening on their own. A few more minutes in the hallway won't hurt him, she decided, and moved from the door.

The sound of heavy footsteps sent her rushing back. They were moving fast, retreating. She flung the door open. He must be running; she could hear him descending the steps at record speed.

"John Rockman, you come back here," she yelled, and hurried for the stairwell.

She heard him cross the entry, his rhythm a purposeful march. She heard him swing open the lobby door, then heard his footsteps disappear. Silence. A loud bang followed, echoing up the staircase, surrounding her with a hollow emptiness. Wanda shivered, wrapped her arms about herself, and stared down the zigzag landings.

What now, smarty? Maybe this was her one chance, and she'd blown it. Would he ever call now? He certainly wouldn't come in person again. But why show up at all if he was going to behave like this?

How dare he come all that way and just leave. He hadn't even waited five minutes before giving up. What was his problem? Didn't getting her back matter? Perhaps he had to rush back to some meeting or other. He probably thought seeing him in person would weaken her, and make it easier to talk her into going back to D.C. Knowing John, he'd calculated it down to the second—two-hour drive, three-minute conversation, one-second kiss and voilà. He would be back in his office without skipping a beat.

"The nerve," she said, spinning around and heading for the apartment.

She noticed roses on the floor. She must have kicked them when she ran out. The box was open, and the red flowers were scattered in front of the open door. Whenever she got angry, John avoided asking why; he sent roses. He always sent twelve red longstems, always from the florist near his office, and always without a card.

Wanda gathered the flowers and the box and went inside. The soft perfume floated around her. She breathed deeply, again and again, until she became light-headed. Same smell. Same florist, she thought, checking the box. She looked inside and out for a card, and shook her head. The same no message, and the same old John.

Yep, she had a lot of work ahead of her, and she'd

start by returning his peace offering. If she hurried, he would get it special delivery.

Clutching the roses in one hand, she rushed across the room to the large window on the front side of the building. Quickly, she raised it and leaned out. Yes, his car was there. She hadn't missed him. Maybe he was still in the first foyer; she didn't remember hearing the street door close. She leaned out as far as safety allowed, holding the roses high, poised and ready.

Behind her the dead bolt clicked noisily. She heard the door swing open. Wanda drew herself in, and slammed the back of her head into the window. The roses tumbled to the sidewalk. She grabbed the base of her neck, and with her eyes half closed, turned and squinted at the figures in the doorway. Dusty stood holding two grocery bags, her head cocked to one side. John had stationed himself just behind her, his arms folded, head tilted in the opposite direction.

"Jumping will solve nothing," he said. "Besides, I understand most people change their minds halfway down."

"If anyone around here goes out this window, it won't be me."

"In case you're interested," said Dusty, "I found him in the foyer, setting up camp, and convinced him he'd be better off up here. So don't make me a liar. No biting his head off, and no tossing him out the window."

"No guarantees," Wanda said.

"Ditto," he answered.

"I see. This is going to be one of those get-down-and-dirty fights," Dusty said. "Then you'll excuse me if I don't stay and watch the blood."

Wanda stood still for a minute, studying him. He looked so baffled. John, a man who hated change and disorder, was experiencing his life turned upside down. Poor baby, she thought. He was trying; he did drive all the way here to see **her**. The tingles erupted again. Wanda felt the warm spot in her center grow hotter, and spread down toward her thighs.

"We have to talk," he said.

"Yes, John." She barely recognized her own whisper. She fought the urge to rush into his arms and murmur, "Take me home."

"Good, we agree. So, let's get started. I told Larry I wouldn't be gone long."

His words sobered her faster than a freezing cold shower.

"Are you sure you can spare the time?"

"Of course. Just tell me what's wrong. We can start now, and finish discussing it on the way home."

"That simple, huh?"

"How complicated can it be? You're mad because I work late."

"That's what all this is about?"

"You think I don't know what's been upsetting you? Don't worry, I almost have the Jackson business settled. After that, my hours will be back to normal."

"Back to normal as in five to nine, or nine to midnight? You haven't a clue," she said, shaking her head and watching John's frown deepen.

"What? Is it something else?"

"It's a lot of something else. We have to start over."

"Okay. I'll start over. I said you're mad because I work late and you said—"

"Not the conversation. Our marriage. We have to start our marriage over."

"What? Why? What did I say? Ahhh. It's the dog thing. You're still mad about the dog."

"No, it's not the dog thing. It's us, and where our lives are headed...or not headed."

"But we have a good life. New house...the firm is doing well. Once I've finished with Jackson, everything will be back on schedule."

"Then what? John, your goal was to build a reputable firm. R and S is that, and more."

"Nothing's stopping us from cornering more of the market. We can be the most prestigious firm in the area—in the nation."

"If we stick to the plan," she said.

"Yes. Why wouldn't we?"

"Because of the cost. Life can't be plotted and charted and long-range forecasted. Life is full of surprises and accidents, and I don't want to be so focused I miss out on them."

"Well, sure, but we can anticipate those—surprises—and deal with them when they arise. We needn't be caught off guard."

Wanda groaned. *Caught off guard?*

"That's the difference, John. You see those things as problems; I see them as spice. And our life—our marriage—lacks spice."

"What is this, a cooking class? Okay, you want spice, we'll have spice. What will it take? An exotic vacation? Tibet. How about Tibet? Or a boat? We can buy a boat...sail the Caribbean. In a few years we can do it, just say the word."

"Baby," she said. She hadn't intended to. That one tiny word always produced the most powerful silences. Wanda held her breath and waited. The heaviness in the room settled on her shoulders, and they slumped without resistance.

"Not that word," he said at last.

"Of course not." She watched him exhale. No, it was too soon to discuss the baby. She had a lot of work to do first.

"We don't need an exotic vacation, but we do need time together without shop talk. The few times we go out are really tax write-offs disguised as dates. I don't know why I bother going. I feel like some tagalong—you talk business with clients and you don't even notice me."

"I love you, Wanda. I respect you...I notice you."

She didn't question his love nor his respect for her. But she couldn't soften now. John needed total reprogramming and the only way to succeed was by introducing her own special virus.

"Close your eyes. Go on, close them. Now, tell me what I have on."

John gnawed on his bottom lip. His brow furrowed. She swore sweat glistened on his forehead.

"This is ridiculous," he said.

"No peeking."

"Pink!" he blurted out.

"Right," Wanda said, looking down at her frumpy blue sweat suit. "Pink is far from my favorite color."

"Pink, blue. That's not the point. I love you. You love me. Right?"

"I'll never stop."

"Then why are we here? Let's go home."

"No. I said we have to start over, and that's what I mean."

"Do we have to start over right here in Dusty's living room? Why can't we start over at home?"

"You know why. I've tried having this conversation before, and every time, where does it lead?"

"To the best room in the house."

Wanda felt her face flush. "Not this time," she said. "You're going home alone, you're going to call me up, and invite me out. We're going to start from scratch...with the first date."

"How can I have a first date with someone I've been married to for ten years?"

"Use your imagination."

"Okay. I call, we *first date,* then what?"

"We take it from there."

"Of all the... Wanda, this is silly. I don't have time to *take it from there.* I have Jackson breathing down my neck. I can't schedule wooing holidays."

"If we are important to you, you'll try."

"Fine. A date you want, a date you'll get. But let's nix this take-it-from-there business here and now. We do this, we set a time period...say two weeks. That's two weekends, six days."

Two weeks. Her mouth went dry. How was she to undo years of conditioning in only two weeks?

"If we can't work this out in two weeks, then we've got a problem dating won't solve," he said.

"Two weeks it is, then." It would be a scramble, but if the spirits could transform Scrooge in one night, she could probably do the same with John in twelve.

"I'll pick you up around five, we'll grab a bite and take in a movie."

"You can't talk at the movies. How about dinner?"

"Where?"

"Surprise me...someplace different."

"Fine. Seven o'clock. One surprise dinner in a spice shop."

John stumped toward the exit, grabbed the knob and swung the door open. She rushed to his side before he could slam it shut and storm away. She removed his hand from the knob and gently squeezed it.

"Thank you for trying this," she said, and felt his tension dissolve.

He drew her to him. Her heart pounded. Every close corner of her body moistened. She felt John harden and press up against her. His hand traced downward, cupping her buttocks, kneading her, pushing her upward and onto him. Her breath caught. She was spinning toward a familiar place, and she couldn't get there fast enough.

"Come home, Wanda," John said, his hoarse voice coming from deep within his throat. "Come home."

"I will."

"Now. Come home now."

Wanda looked up into his eyes. Something calculated hid behind their twinkle. If she went home now their lives would never change.

His lips parted and lowered toward hers. Wanda raised her fingers in time, but he sucked them into his mouth, and teased them with little licks and nibbles.

"I'll come home," she said, removing her hand and easing him away. "But first...our date."

"The date," he said, nuzzling the top of her head.

"Uh-huh. And it has to be a good date."

"Oh, it will be one enchanted evening."

"Good. Until then." She stepped back, ready to close the door.

"How about a good-night kiss?"

"Next time," she whispered, looking up at him. He pouted, faking a hurt expression. "I'll wait for your call," she said. She was sure her face was flushed and that he could hear the desire in her voice. He knew just what he was doing to her.

"I know," he answered with a smirk, and started for the stairs.

"John," she called after him. "Remember what happened the very first night we went out?"

He turned, looking puzzled.

"Nothing. Absolutely nothing, because I said, 'No.'"

And she closed the door.

3

—————

THE RESTAURANT had not opened for dinner, but it bustled with life. Waiters rushed about setting tables; shouts escaped the kitchen area, as did tantalizing aromas of basil, onion and garlic.

A large arrangement of tropical flowers decorated the foyer where John stood. Yes this was the perfect spot for spice.

He looked down at the maitre d', a trim man reaching no higher than John's shoulder and wearing his authority like a banner on a beauty queen.

"You have already checked these details via phone. It was not necessary to check in person," the man explained.

"Occupational habit," John said. "I'm sure your restaurant, with its reputation for customer satisfaction, won't mind going over them a second time."

"Third. Very well. Reservations for two are set for seven forty-five sharp. Why? Because you are picking up your date at seven o'clock and your drive across town will take exactly forty-two minutes." The man couldn't have looked more sour even with a mouthful of unripe persimmons.

"I timed it," John said.

"No doubt under varying weather conditions. You will have a table which affords privacy. Your champagne and menus will arrive right after you are seated, and your waiter, ten minutes after that.

"And the—"

"Two bottles are already chilling. We do have everything under control. I hope you see no need to check any further...say with the chef, or your waiter."

John's jaw muscles twitched, but he kept his expression neutral. Not since his youth, his years of poverty, had he been treated so curtly. He'd come a long way from the back alleys of Baltimore, but the stinging memories remained fresh.

He had a good mind to accept the caustic offer. Instead, he reached into his pants pocket, palmed the tip he had ready, and shook the maitre d's hand. The bill passed smoothly from one to the other.

"And what is this?" the man asked.

"We tend to get a bit rowdy. I want to cover any damage in advance."

The expression on the man's face was worth it, he thought as he walked away, leaving the maitre d' standing openmouthed and pale.

This would be one expensive date, he thought as he drove across town. The dinner would easily set him back a hundred dollars or more. His hotel suite was twice that per day.

Yes, he'd come a long way from his childhood days living in hostels and hippie camps with his mother, and later hustling crap games for grocery money. His life experience had taught him well. He would always have a long-term plan.

Direction and discipline did not spell rigidity. Maybe that's why Wanda didn't understand; her background was so opposite his. Once he got her back home, he'd work on making her see the difference. But first, the lady would have her spice.

He parked outside of Dusty's apartment building and sat thinking. He'd give her spice all right. Dinner at the best place in town, one glass of wine over her two-drink limit, then off to the hotel where he'd booked a suite for the weekend. Telling the staff it was their honeymoon was a stroke of genius. Champagne and flowers would be awaiting them. She'd get her spice, all right, and more. After the night of passion he had planned, she would never complain again.

He smiled at the image of Wanda, exhausted from lovemaking, her hair spread erotically over her pillow, her naked body, half-covered by crumpled sheets and glistening with sweat. He thought of all the things he would do to her, do with her, to get her in that state.

Suddenly his stomach tightened. A warmth flooded through him. He floated on a tide, his center undulating to its rhythm. He felt himself harden. A few deep breaths stilled the flood. Slowly the throbbing pressure eased also. Patience. Two hours of Wanda's ritual courtship, and on to the real agenda.

He'd resented her idea, at first. Now he was looking forward to this "date." John checked his appearance. The tailor-made tux still fit to a tee, and his bow tie was straight. His shoes had a high polish, even though they pinched his toes slightly. What did it matter? They wouldn't be dancing. His plans called for their feet to be off the floor and bare. A smile swept his whole body.

"Okay, Wanda, here I come," he said, jumping out of the car and taking the front steps two at a time.

John paused outside Dusty's door, checked his tie again, and smoothed his lapels. What would she say when she saw him in this? Nothing like a little elegance to make a woman's heart skip a beat.

He put on his best innocent smile, rang the bell, and waited. And waited. He rang it again, this time keeping his thumb in place for a good ten seconds, then waited some more.

Wanda was playing games again. But panic rushed in. Did he have the right day, the right time? This was certainly the right apartment. Just as he raised his fist to pound, the door opened.

Dusty jumped backward.

"Whoa, take it easy," she said, ducking.

"Sorry. I was—"

"Hoping for Wanda? Don't worry, I know the feeling." Dusty eyed his fist.

She stepped aside and he entered. He watched her smile widen. She looked him up and down, then released a slow whistle.

"Approve?"

"What's not to approve?"

"Is she ready?"

"Depends upon your perspective. I'll get her, and you decide for yourself." Dusty backed out of the room, staring at him until she disappeared down the hall.

"John has come a-courting," he heard her yell. Low chatter and giggles followed.

First date jitters. He didn't expect that of Wanda, but it pleased him. He walked to the window and looked out. The evening was perfect, the sky clear and sprinkled with stars. If this was D.C., he would take her on a postdinner, romantic spin around the Tidal Basin, but here in Richmond he was at a loss. Perhaps Dusty would have some suggestions. Something to get Wanda in the mood—an overture to the honeymoon suite.

He was deep in thought when he heard heavy heels clomp into the room.

"My, Dusty was right. You do look pretty," Wanda said, letting the last word roll around her tongue in a drawl.

John turned and gaped. She had on black boots with silver toes, black jeans spray-paint-tight, and a red gingham shirt opened two buttons too low. She stood with a hand on her hip, her wild mane falling over her face. She was one bad cowgirl, looking too darn good.

"You're...you're not ready."

"Sure I am." She pushed her hair back. Her turquoise eyes twinkled. It struck him how bright they were. When she was upset, they clouded to the milky likeness of the stone. Tonight, they shone like the Caribbean Sea.

"I made reservations at a four-star restaurant. They'll never let you in dressed like that!"

"That's fine. I have someplace else in mind."

"Where, a ranch? I made reservations for the best spot in town, because *you* suggested dinner."

"*You* just don't know every spot in this town. Besides, I suggested a surprise."

"You said, 'Surprise me.' Not the other way around."

"You need the practice, though. Are you ready for some down-home cooking and country dancing?"

"Look at me. I can't go country-and-western dancing."

"Why not? Shoes too tight?"

John threw up his arms. Dealing with Wanda was never easy.

"Look how I'm dressed," he said.

"You look real good to me, like some slick river-boat gambler."

"Perfect," he said, sarcastically.

"You smell good, too." Wanda's nose traced his chest, and sent hot quivers flowing in its wake.

He looked down at the top of her head, and fought to keep his hands at his side instead of tangled in the mass of shiny curls. *Who was seducing whom?* He held his breath and counted to ten. He'd reached fifty before realizing she was talking to him.

"...flexibility, spontaneity, spice, remember? Come on John, it's our first date. You said you'd try. Besides, you'll fit in better at Lone Ranger's than I would at some fancy restaurant."

He looked into her upturned face. So they would have ribs and beer instead of lobster and champagne. The evening would still end as he planned—back at his suite with its king-size bed.

"Fine, flexible you want, flexible it is. Lead me to the hoedown."

"You're getting the hang of it." Wanda reached up, locked her arms around his neck, kissed his cheek, and was halfway across the living room when she said, "Now if Dusty would just hurry up."

"Dusty? She's not coming." He remembered she had on a similar outfit, but hadn't made the connection.

"Of course she's coming. You should never go out alone on a first date."

"Of course," he said. *What's a date without the cavalry?*

"I'm ready." Dusty entered the room. She was a carbon copy of Wanda, except her hair was pulled back under a black, wide-brimmed hat.

Now he had two bad cowgirls. He just hoped the cowboys at Lone Ranger's were nothing like the rowdy men he'd seen in the movies. He was in no mood to ride to the ladies' rescue.

"Ladies," he said, offering each an elbow.

"We can't leave yet," Dusty said. "We have to wait for Charlie."

"Who?"

Just then the front bell sounded. Wanda opened the door, linked arms with the mustached man standing there and spun him down the hall before John could blink.

"Meet Charlie," Dusty said, leading John out of the apartment. "You can close your mouth—he's my date."

"For some reason, that gives no comfort."

"Huh. You're catching on," she replied. "Relax, it can only get worse."

"*That* I know all too well." He just hoped the night in his suite would make it all worth the trouble.

A green pickup, double parked next to his Honda, idled loudly. John stopped walking and eyed it. Just how far was Wanda going to go, and how far did she expect him to play along?

"Hop in," said Dusty, pointing to the flatbed.

The bed, as rusted as the rest of the truck, offered a hay bale as seating.

"Should I ask what he usually carries back here?"

"Nope. You don't want to know."

Before the two of them could settle atop the bale of hay, the truck took off with a roar and sped down the street. Dusty held on to her hat; John held on to the side of the truck.

Soon the city disappeared, replaced by a country landscape. The roads got more winding and rougher, but Charlie drove faster. John pitched from one side of the truck to the other.

"Where'd this guy learn to drive, the circus?"

"Charlie's a good driver. You got any complaints, take them up with Wanda. She's behind the wheel."

And she's doing this on purpose, he thought, but said, "She drives just like she thinks, too fast and too reckless."

"I for one, think you're a real sport to put up with all this. You must really love her."

"Not as much as I did twenty minutes ago."

Suddenly the truck jerked to a stop, and the two passengers landed on the floor. John raised himself on his hands, leaned over the tailgate, and stared across the parking lot at a red barnlike structure.

He spied Wanda and Charlie running across the lot. They disappeared through big, double doors emitting loud music that spilled out and filled the night with its steady beat. Everything, the trees, the truck, John's insides, moved to the thumping rhythm. It wasn't the music, he realized, but the dancing, stomping feet of hundreds of cow-folk that stirred the surroundings.

He glanced at the barn's second-story loft area. A horse and rider, outlined in a string of white lights, blinked off and on as they bucked and reared in place. Just above them was a big neon sign proclaiming the place Lone Ranger's.

He jumped to the ground, removed his jacket, stuffed his tie and cummerbund in the pocket, and undid three shirt buttons.

"How's this look?" he asked Dusty, after helping her down.

"Do you have to wear those things?" She pointed to his glasses.

He shrugged, folded the glasses, and placed them in his pocket. "Nothing else about this evening is in focus."

She stepped back, studying him the same way he scrutinized his designs. Finally she removed her hat, and placed it on his head at a jaunty angle.

"It's too big for me, anyway," she explained. "You know, every third set ends with ladies' choice. A man armed with that kind of information can give his date something to worry about. Just make sure you're standing near the big doors where all the unattached women hang out."

"I thought you were in on Wanda's little scheme."

"I'm in, all right. The whole idea behind this evening was for you to experience something different, and have fun, to boot. I bet you've danced all night with a room full of pretty women."

"I bet that's not what Wanda had in mind."

"She suggested a surprise. Maybe this one will teach her to think things through before acting."

"You're on my side. You see what I've been dealing with."

"Whoa, boy. I see what you both have been dealing with. A little changing won't hurt either of you. Let's say I'm for a more perfect union."

He'd expected her to side completely with Wanda. That she was trying to see both views spoke well of his sister-in-law.

"Then wish me luck," he said, offering his arm.

"I wish you both luck. I just hope that's enough."

So do I, he thought as they walked into the dance hall.

Lone Ranger's was what he expected: sawdust on the floor, pitchers of beer on heavy, wooden tables, cowgirl waitresses. Wall lamps made from longhorns and antlers added atmosphere. Everything else was state-of-the-art, from the large oval bar and the dance floor washed in theater lights, to the ultraloud sound system.

The four of them huddled around a table, a platter of naked rib bones and two empty beer pitchers before them.

"Don't forget to save me a dance," Dusty shouted in his direction before rushing onto the dance floor with Charlie.

He had no intention of going out there. For one thing, he didn't have a clue what the people on the floor were doing. He was fine with a fox-trot and could spin a decent waltz, but this was like some ritual dance of an unknown tribe.

He didn't mind the music, though. He was content sitting and listening, but Wanda tapped his shoulder and nodded toward the floor. John smiled and shook his head.

"It's just a two-step," she shouted.

"Can't hear you," he pretended.

"Two-step. You know." She demonstrated with her fingers.

He bit his bottom lip, holding back a laugh. "Oh a two-step, I see."

Wanda beamed, stood and held out her hand. He shook his head again. "I don't like the two-step," he said.

She flopped back into her chair, and crossed her

arms over her chest, an act that pushed her breast outward. Good, let her stew a bit, he thought, but found himself staring at her soft curves and longing to touch them. He pulled his focus away, smiled brightly and held up the pitcher, signaling a waitress.

A tall brunette approached the table. Her jeans were as tight as Wanda's, her hair as long, but her blouse was definitely more open. He noticed his wife sitting taller and glaring in the woman's direction.

"A refill, please." He used his deepest voice.

"If I see your waitress, I'll pass on the request. In the meantime, you care to dance?"

The band had finished its number, and was starting something new. John noticed the lights dim.

"It's not ladies' choice." Wanda frowned and jutted her chin.

"I'm not much for ceremony." The brunette looked at John when she talked.

"That's obvious. But you can find somebody else? He doesn't dance."

"It's okay. This is a waltz...I like waltzes," John said.

He let the woman lead him onto the floor, but once there, he held her close and spun off, careful to stay on the periphery of the crowd. Every few turns, he would steal a glance toward the table to make sure Wanda was watching. She was, and from what he could see she was also fuming.

She pulled on her hair, twisted in her chair, folded and unfolded her arms. She drummed the table to a beat other than three-fourths time. He noticed that all through her fidgeting, she kept her focus on him and his partner, but when he returned to the table, she gave a start, as though his arrival surprised her.

"Since when did you become such a country-and-western fan?"

"Can't hear you," he shouted over the music.

"You heard *her* all right. 'You care to dance?' It's just me you can't hear."

"Beer? That waitress will never come. I'll go get it myself." He escaped with the empty pitchers.

When he returned, he filled both their glasses, toasted the air and drank heartily. The emcee announced the next dance and John turned to face Wanda.

"This one is ladies' choice," he said.

"So."

"Aren't you going to make your choice?"

"And I suppose you think you're it. Well, don't hold your breath."

"Come on Wanda, it's our first date. Please try."

"It's a two-step—you don't like the two-step."

"You don't have to do that if you don't want," a redheaded cowgirl interrupted. "I can show you another dance."

"Wanda?" John asked with raised eyebrows.

"Seems it's husband season. Help yourself—he's game."

John stood, then leaned and whispered in her ear. "Must be the suit," he said.

Four songs later, he was still on the floor. He was getting the hang of the complicated line dances when he looked over and found his table empty. He scanned the room, spotted Wanda slipping out the front door and hurried after her.

She was crossing the parking lot, headed for the truck.

"Wanda!"

She answered with bouncing curls and silence.

John ran and jumped into the truck seconds before she drove off. He knew better than to speak, so he watched the road, and occasionally glanced at her profile. She was mad, all right. Her mouth was set and the muscles in her jaw twitched. Her hands gripped the wheel so hard, her knuckles whitened. *Jealous.*

Until tonight, he never truly worried about Wanda's driving. Now her foot pressed too heavily upon the gas pedal, and they sped down the road, hitting every bump along the way. The hay bale had made a better seat. At least when he bounced, he didn't hit his head.

"Don't they give speeding tickets down here, or don't you care?"

"I don't stand on ceremony," she answered.

"Fair enough," he said. "Just where are we going?"

"I'm going to the river. Since you're sitting here, I guess you're going, too."

"I stop at jumping in. If you have that in mind, it's a solo act."

"Suit yourself."

They continued the rest of the way in silence, until she finally pulled off the road, drove over a grassy stretch and jammed on the brakes. The James River sparkled before them. John rolled down the windows and listened to the night music of the crickets and frogs. He had wanted a romantic spot for their after dinner drive. Wanda had solved the problem. Unfortunately, she was far from being in a romantic mood.

"I'm sorry the evening didn't turn out well. Guess this wasn't your idea of spice."

"More like pepper," she said.

"We can try again, tomorrow."

"Why bother? You did that on purpose."

"What? You intentionally mislead me...suggest dinner, then drag me off to a hoedown, and I'm at fault?"

"You seemed to enjoy yourself, Mr. Twinkle Toes. Someone must have put a burr in your patent leather shoes."

"Don't be jealous."

"Jealous. I'm mad. Four dances with Big Red, and not one of them a waltz."

"She's the owner. We were talking about the barn. She told me all about the renovations. She wants to make more changes, so I gave her a few suggestions. We'll meet next month, formally."

"Oh, so it was business. You saved your receipts? You can use the whole evening with Wanda as another tax write-off. How convenient."

Why was she so hard to please?

"Would you prefer we had talked about something else—the full moon, for instance?"

"There is no full moon," she said.

Hang in there, Rocko. "I'm sorry, Wanda."

"You should be."

He thought he heard less of an edge to her voice.

"I was lost in there...the wrong clothes, didn't know the dances. I was the oddball. Some of the women thought that charming, but not the one who mattered."

Wanda opened her mouth and slowly shut it. The lines in her face softened and her eyes glistened.

Meltdown. He traced her lips with his fingertips.

"You ignored me the entire night," she said.

"I told you before, I never ignore you." He continued tracing her lips. "Even when I'm at work, you're on my mind. I never ignore you."

Wanda batted his hand away and retreated to her corner. Why had he mentioned work? Now he had to start over.

"Don't ignore me, huh." She snorted. "Close your eyes."

"Again?"

"Yes, again. Now, what am I wearing?"

"A cowgirl outfit."

"Brilliant. What type of cowgirl outfit...and don't peek."

John took a deep breath. How was he to remember that? All he was sure of was the walloping impact it had made on his senses. He took another deep breath and reached out toward her.

"Hey," she protested, but didn't push his hands away.

He touched her knees and slowly traveled upward.

"Jeans," he said, "tight jeans."

He moved up her thigh, following the inseam. When he reach the point where the seams met, he heard her gasp.

"*Very* tight jeans," he said, massaging the area. Wanda pressed forward into his hands. He heard her breathing grow irregular, and he moved his hands upward.

"A very thin blouse, open at the neck," he whispered while undoing a few more buttons.

"John." Her voice was weak, and so was her resistance, he calculated.

"It's okay. My eyes are still closed. I'm not peeking."

But his hands were busy. He slid one inside her shirt and cupped her breast. She moaned loudly when he took the nipple between thumb and forefinger and gently rubbed. "No bra...you never wear a bra."

He kissed her then, on each taut nipple, and traveled downward licking every inch of exposed skin. He would have preferred the king-size bed back at the hotel, but he knew he couldn't wait. The little sounds she made echoed in his head; his ears burned. His heart beat rapidly, his stomach tightened, and his entire body felt electrified, but it all seemed to concentrate in one place. There he hardened, trying to push free of his pants. He had never made out in a car, but there was always a first time.

John continued kissing until his head was nestled in her lap. The smell of her—the hot, musky mix of perfume and woman—was more than he could bear.

"Now, Wanda...right here...right now."

"Yes, John," she said. Her voice sounded unusually clear. She stiffened under him.

Suddenly the truck shot backward. John hit his head on the steering wheel and fell to the floor. He scrambled into his seat and stared at her.

"There are just some things I don't do on a first date, so right here, right now, I say no."

HE STOOD BESIDE his car and watched her drive away. The truck's exhaust filled his nose and mixed with the bitter taste in his mouth. His throat tightened on reflex. He would *not* be sick. He'd be angry, frustrated, hurt but not sick. John balled his hands into fists, and shook them in the air. He wanted to scream, to curse, to...

"Ugh!" He howled with his face raised skyward,

turning a circle as he screamed. "Ugh," he cried again, and kicked his car's tire.

Pain shot from his toe up his leg. He fell against the car, holding his foot and ankle. Why beat himself up; hadn't she done enough to him already?

So much for taming her with a night of passion. That tactic had always worked before; he couldn't understand why it hadn't this time. She'd certainly seemed eager, then wham, the polar freeze. Had he moved too quickly?

He hobbled into the car, and started across town determined he'd have it all analyzed by the time he reached the hotel. Before he knew it, he was back in his room asking the same question. Had he moved too quickly?

Probably. For a first date he'd come on like a pawing lecher—Casanova with a stopwatch. The setting hadn't helped, either. An angry, jealous woman wouldn't appreciate making out in a pickup, no matter how wide the seats.

He'd calculated right the first time. This situation called for soft lights, champagne and a real bed. The suite had a king-size one, but size didn't matter unless he got her in it. To do that, he would have to slow down, stay calm, be subtle.

A night of lovemaking would remind her of the magic between them, that special something that told them both they were meant for each other forever and always.

John crawled into bed, and pulled the covers over his head. Tomorrow. They had another date planned for tomorrow. Wanda had promised no tricks. He wished he could believe that. Whatever her scheme,

he would play along, and somehow maneuver her
back to his suite.

Nothing tricky about that.

WANDA SAT IN the middle of the bed in the guest
room, her arms wrapped around her legs, her chin
resting on her knees. John's shirt, one of three she
hadn't shipped to his office, covered her, muumuu
style. It was almost 2 A.M. She should just forget trying to fall asleep.

What happened? How did things turn so upside
down? She started out in total control. John had been
thrown by the change in plans, but he behaved like a
trouper, showing the flexibility and spontaneity he
needed so much more of.

She had every intention of calling it quits before
he got too uncomfortable. Instead, the tables turned.
She was the uncomfortable one. Who would have
guessed he'd be the answer to every cowgirl's dream.

That he answered all her dreams was no surprise.
It was no surprise that when he touched her, everything deep inside stirred. He knew what he did to her,
and he knew how to do it: his tongue, his kisses, not
devouring, but caressing, gently brushing her hot
spots. Tasting, teasing until she could stand no more,
until all she wanted was to pull his mouth onto hers,
press his body closer, and draw him inside.

She was at that point in the truck when she remembered. She was unprotected. As much as she wanted
a baby, she would not have one this way. John must
agree. He must want a child as much as she did, and
be ready to give that child his time and attention.

She was thankful she stopped when she did, even
though her actions had left John stunned. What must

he think of her now? That she was jealous and spiteful? Probably. How could she prove otherwise when his slightest touch made her lose control?

From now on, she must keep him at arm's length, and she had to accomplish that without seeming cold and disinterested. She could establish a no-touch rule, but neither of them were beyond breaking it.

No, she needed a backup system—something, or someone to sound a retreat when every passionate pore of hers screamed charge. She'd better think fast. They had another date tomorrow, and she was determined not to let that one get out of control.

She should never have taken him to Lone Ranger's; the setting was all wrong. A loud country-and-western bar was perfect for introducing John to a fun, new environment, but it did nothing to reinforce the pleasures of family life and sharing. No, they needed a calmer setting, minus all those single, obliging cowgirls. She knew just the spot.

A smile spread across her face as she visualized the upcoming date. This time she would call John and let him know exactly where they were going. No more tricks would be her new motto. Surprises, yes. John's stuffy armor still needed a few more surprise attacks. But there would certainly be no more tricks. Fortunately, there was nothing tricky about this new plan. Nothing at all.

4

"I HAVEN'T DONE THIS in ages," Wanda said, lacing her fingers through John's and giving his hand a little squeeze. She looked up at the old magnolias lining the path. Their green, waxy leaves contrasted sharply with the red and yellow maple ones that rustled in the sudden breeze.

The afternoon sun was a dazzling gold color. Later it would diffuse into hues of orange and purple and wash the sky with its setting glow. For now, Wanda lifted her face, savoring the waning warmth.

Sunday in the park with John. No reservations needed, no schedule, no business associates tagging along. Nothing planned beyond arriving, walking and enjoying.

The breeze intensified, reminding her that winter's chill was only months away. She shivered, snuggling deeper into her sweater and closer to John.

"Cold?" He wrapped his arms around her. The picnic basket he held bumped into her back. "We'll leave now if you're cold."

She shook her head, ignoring the hopeful tone in his voice. She wouldn't let a little breeze spoil what was to be a perfect date in her favorite park. As a child, she had come here with her mother and Dusty.

Her father never joined them. A devout workaholic, his career took precedence over family activities. His efforts earned them an upper-middle-class life-style, but Wanda eventually realized he worked for himself and not them, as he claimed. His job defined him, giving him a sense of accomplishment and pleasure his family never could. Perhaps it was a blessing he'd died at his desk while his coworkers celebrated his retirement.

And now, John was acting more and more like her father with each passing workday, but she would save him before it was too late. Hopefully, this little outing would open his eyes to what they were missing. If being surrounded by happy families had no effect on him, she didn't know what would.

She had packed John's favorite foods, and the weather was chilly but passable. Now, to find the perfect picnic spot.

"There," she said, pointing to a sunny meadow. "We'll spread out down there."

A number of families obviously had the same idea. Their colorful blankets spotted the grass; their happy voices sounded a welcome. It was a scene right out of a photo album. She smiled, observing fathers playing catch with their sons, mothers tending babies, children running, laughing, and a dog chasing a Frisbee. The perfect spot, she thought, tugging at John's arm.

He didn't budge.

"It's already crowded," he said.

"No, it isn't," she said and pulled until he followed with stiff-legged acceptance.

"It's noisy."

"Come on." She led the way into the family circus.

"Tables." He stood aside watching her spread the

blanket. "There're no picnic tables. I can't eat sitting on the ground. My legs will go to sleep."

"Where do you suppose they ate?" she asked, giving the area a grand sweep with her arm.

"Anyone with respect for chilly weather, cold grounds, and long legs would eat at home, at a dinner table."

Without commenting, Wanda laid out the food, and using measured movements, peeled the tops off each container. First, she uncovered the chicken she had fried that morning. The aroma, as tantalizing as when she'd packed it three hours ago, filled the air. Next she unveiled the potato salad, the still-warm rolls, and last, the chocolate cake. She didn't wait for him; she filled a plate and dug in.

John leaned forward, swaying like a sapling in a strong wind. Good, she thought, let his senses take over. They'll teach that stuffy brain of his a thing or two.

"Delicious," she said in between bites, and patted the blanket next to her.

John folded himself onto the ground, squirmed, shifted from one hip to the other, and finally settled on a cross-legged position. A nature boy he wasn't, she thought, observing how awkward he looked, but she, too, squirmed when her faded jeans bit into her thigh. *Must cut down on the ice cream.*

"Did you bring anything to drink?" John asked, after helping himself to food.

"Hot coffee. The thermos is in there."

His straight shoulders sank when she indicated the picnic basket sitting more than an arm's length away on the edge of the blanket.

"I put it there to keep the blanket from flying up," she explained.

"Not to aid the ants—decrease their toting distance when they decide to cart the food away?"

Wanda rolled her eyes, but secretly hoped the ants remained underground. If a few ants appeared, John would declare the spot infested, and end their picnic. She peered at him. He had stretched his legs and was biting into the chicken. He even smiled as he chewed. When he looked out over the landscape, she relaxed, but then he glanced at his watch.

"Let's set some ground rules right now," she said, giving him a stern look. "There will be no clock watching during this picnic."

"Okay." His tone sounded too nonchalant for her.

"Fork it over." She held out her palm and waited. Finally he removed the watch and held it above her hand.

"It's not an amputation, just a temporary separation," she said.

He let go and it landed in her palm. It was heavy and still warm from his body. She folded her hand and absorbed the watch's heat, then placed it on the blanket with the face turned away from him. She didn't put it past John to sneak an occasional peek, and she wanted to make the maneuver as awkward for him as possible.

Even without his watch, his attention strayed. His eyes stared vacantly past the landscape. His face suddenly became lined and he pressed his lips together. She could almost hear his brain gears grinding.

"John, you're distracted. You're not even trying to enjoy yourself."

"It's just—"

"Jackson," she answered, and sighed when he nodded.

Of course. He was thinking of work.

How could anyone be focused to the point of such extreme tunnel vision? How unhealthy. He was definitely a prime candidate for a heart attack, just as her father had been. The thought frightened her.

Suddenly her chest felt weighted. She blinked back the pressure forming behind her eyes, and put on a stern face.

"I take it he's nixed another design," she said, trying to hide the anxiety in her voice.

"Nixing alone wouldn't be so bad—I've had ideas vetoed before. The problem is I haven't a clue what Jackson wants. He's constantly changing his mind just like…a…ah…"

"Woman?" She finished the sentence, and sighed when he gave her a you-said-it, raised-eyebrow look. "Since he's so much like a woman, perhaps a woman can offer a few suggestions."

"Doubt it," he said absently, brushing the subject off and staring once more into the distance.

Her throat tightened.

Don't take it personally, she thought, yet found that hard to do. She realized his response said more about his own insecurities than his assessment of her usefulness. Offering help was akin to criticizing his work. He had long ago stopped sharing his design ideas with her, about the same time he had started designing boxes. Still, the comment hurt.

Well, I won't let this day go sour. She looked around for something to draw his attention and chose the scenery. No architect could ignore this setting, not even one who wished he was elsewhere.

"Look at this park," she said. "Lovely. Come on, you must admit it." She scanned the site. "The trees are beautiful, the sun warm. It's so...so..."

She stopped midsentence. John was back to his squirming. He unfolded himself, stretched out first on his left side, then swung around and switched to his right. The blanket pulled and twisted with his every move.

"Please stop," she said.

He refolded himself, ending back where he had started, cross-legged and looking uncomfortable.

When he started the cycle over again, she snapped. "Stop that squirming. You look like a dog in a thorn bush."

"If it's a long-legged dog, I sympathize. Ever notice people who enjoy sitting on the ground are all under five-eight?"

"You'd probably be more comfortable if you didn't wear business clothes everywhere," she said, pointing to his dark gray slacks, blue sport coat and white shirt.

When not in a gray suit, that combination substituted as his standard fare. She hated those colors.

"This isn't business. Only with a tie would this qualify as business."

"Well it's certainly not a picnic."

"I wasn't thinking picnic when I rushed down from D.C."

"Who told you to rush?" she asked, remembering the shock of finding him at Dusty's door.

"Who told me? I came home to no home. I would call that scenario borderline urgent. I rushed. Sue me for not remembering picnic clothes."

His eyes glared like headlights from behind his

glasses. The vein in his temple beat against his skin. She wanted him to show some feeling, but anger was not the emotion of choice.

She wasn't helping, though, going tit for tat the way she was. She closed her eyes and took two cleansing breaths.

"Let's not fight. Let's enjoy this day."

"Let's," he said, tight-voiced. He grabbed a drumstick and tore the meat from the bone. "Let's," he repeated with full mouth and exaggerated chewing.

"I'm sorry. It's just... Well, anyone would think you were born with a suit coat on. You don't even own a pair of jeans. You used to, but you let them dry-rot in the closet. You're always so formal."

"This is not formal. Yesterday was formal."

She blushed, remembering how handsome he looked in his tuxedo, but the tint vanished quickly. What did it matter how handsome he looked when he had focused all his attention on the bar owner and business?

"At least yesterday you took off your jacket."

"*Yesterday* I wasn't outside picnicking in forty-degree weather."

"It's fifty-five and sunny. But if you're so cold," she said, filling a paper cup with coffee, "here."

She placed the drink beside him without checking for a level spot. The cup rocked. She watched the slow-motion teetering, half wishing the liquid would spill all over his clean, creased pants.

Her wish came true. The cup rocked toward him and tipped, splashing hot, black liquid everywhere.

He jerked to attention, then froze, his mouth open in a silent scream.

Guilt washed over her. He was in pain and it was her fault for wishing it.

"Take that off—the sleeve is soaked. Oh, your slacks!" Using the one dry sleeve, she wiped his pants with the sport jacket.

He remained stone frozen. She was aware of his frosty stare, so intense she could almost feel it bore a hole into the top of her head. She could also sense his pain, as keenly as if she, too, were burned, but she knew better than to try to comfort him. Experience had taught her he preferred his cuts and scrapes neat and straight up—no first aid, no bandages and certainly no kisses.

"There," she said, placing the jacket down and picking up a paper plate. "How about some more chicken?"

"How about leaving before things get worse." There was no asking in his tone, she noticed.

"Don't be a party poop. We've had our disaster. What more could happen?" Once spoken, she wanted to snatch the words back and swallow them.

Too late.

From the corner of her eye, she spied a bright, neon green satellite zeroing in on her head. She ducked just as the disk dived. It smacked her nose, bounced off, and landed in the chocolate cake.

She wasn't sure which hurt more, witnessing the bomb attack on their dessert or the piercing ache spreading across the bridge of her nose. She didn't have time to decide. From nowhere, a shaggy brown dog traipsed over the blanket and proceeded to paw the cake. Its long tail fanned Wanda's face.

"I want my Frisbee back." A little boy scowled at her, his lower lip thrust out. She guessed he was four or five, certainly too young to have perfected accurate aim. Under any other circumstances, she would probably think him cute.

With thumb and forefinger, she eased the toy out of the chocolate layer mess. The dog, undisturbed by her action, continued to feast.

"It's dirty," the boy protested when she offered it to him.

Wanda looked and spied John hiding his jacket behind his back. She found a napkin and wiped the green disc as clean as possible before presenting it again. The boy snatched his prize. He gave her a long child's stare she had difficulty returning.

"Run along," she said, but he didn't move. "Go on." She was beginning to squirm under his scrutiny. "Aaahh!" she screamed in frustration, wagging her tongue and crossing her eyes.

"Mamma!" came the child's answering cry as he ran away.

The dog zipped after him, bounding into Wanda, knocking her off balance. She pitched forward into the dish of potato salad. The mush oozed through her fingers, and plastered her chest like cold paste.

"Dogs." John shook his head sympathetically, but she didn't miss the smirk on his face. "There's nothing more appealing than kids and dogs."

"Not that kid, and certainly not that dog. And don't you dare laugh; just give me something to wipe this off."

"That poses a problem. The dog ate the napkins right after he finished the cake. My pants and jacket have already been used." He lifted a corner of the picnic blanket. "Here. Compliments of the house."

She heard him, but she wasn't listening. She stared

beyond him at the blanket and the growing wet spot. The thermos lay on its side, coffee spilling over John's watch. He snatched it up and pressed it to his ear.

"Is it working?" she asked, already knowing the answer. Her voice was so quiet she hardly recognized it. He glared at her, wiped the watch on his jacket and stuffed it into his pants pocket.

It was no use. She had hoped taking John on this picnic, exposing him to the life-style of normal families, would prove so pleasant, he would reevaluate his own perspective. Just her luck. This picnic turned out to be a disaster al fresco.

As she surveyed the damage, a tightness formed in her throat, warning her of the tears building to flood level. She swallowed hard and fought them back.

"Okay. It was a stupid idea," she said, "but I thought you'd get something out of a day like this."

"I got a lot out of it. Believe me." His eyes narrowed as he focused on her. "How much research did you do to find this place?" he asked.

"Research?"

"It fits with all your recent thematic material—crying babies, little kids...dogs."

Heat crept up her neck. The urge to cry suddenly incinerated. She breathed slowly while counting to ten, but couldn't stop the fire from traveling to her face and collecting in her cheeks.

Research. Even if it was somewhat true, how dare he act so put out? She was working to save him, to save their marriage. He just wasn't getting it.

She threw the smashed container of potato salad into the wicker basket and the contents hit with a splat and spread on the bottom. The chicken pieces tumbled one over the other when she pitched them in. Then she tossed the rolls atop the helter-skelter mixture and smirked as they fell into the empty corners. Finally she lifted the chocolate pancake and paused.

"Dessert?" she asked, pushing it under John's nose.

When he backed away, she slammed the cake atop the potpourri, grabbed an end of the blanket, and not waiting for him to stand, yanked with all her strength. John unwrapped his long legs without a hitch and scrambled to his feet.

"I declare this outing over!" she said, balling the blanket into a lumpy roll. When she finished, she punched the material into the basket and forced the top closed. "If you don't mind, please bring the thermos." With that, she marched away.

She didn't turn and check to see if he was following. Instead, she slowed her pace and hoped her march didn't look too much like what it was, stomping in place. She strained, listening for his footsteps, but couldn't hear a thing over the din of the picnickers. *He was right. This spot is noisy,* she thought and about-faced. She jumped.

John stood right in front of her, so close they almost touched—her face to his chest. It was such a wide chest, even his conservative white shirt couldn't disguise his athletic build. She stared at him a second too long before pulling her focus away. When she looked up, she found him studying her.

"How's the nose?" he asked.

"Rearranged. How does it look?"

"Not bad for amateur cosmetic surgery."

She fought the urge, but gave in and caressed the spot where the Frisbee had whacked her. It didn't feel broken. At least they wouldn't be a look-alike couple with matching crooked snouts.

"I hope today and yesterday have taught you something," he said.

"Like what?"

"Like this dating idea of yours is ridiculous and—"

"Ridiculous?"

"*And* you'd better stop before you create more problems than you think you started with."

Wanda inhaled. She would burst from frustration. He stood there, arms folded over his chest, his jaw set. Everything about him remained so set. She wanted to shake him, loosen him up, but she now knew that wouldn't work.

What had Granny said? "You can't shake a scared cat out of a tree. You either chop the damn thing down, or you climb up there and coax him out."

Since sparring had gotten her nowhere, she decided to give Granny's method a try, not that she expected coaxing would be any easier.

"John, I love you," she said. "I don't want to lose you, but I feel I am."

"That's ridiculous. Have I deserted you? Have I hinted, said anything?"

"Not in that way. I'm losing the man I married. That bright-eyed idealist, that gutsy guy who challenged the status quo."

"Good God, Wanda. I grew up. You can't spend your life pulling bricks out of the wall—it'll tumble on you. Pretty soon, a wise man wakes up and realizes if he ever hopes to reach his goal, he has to go with the current, not against it. And that's me—a wise man. I'm building...I'm achieving."

"You've overachieving, and now you're in a rut like a hamster on an exercise wheel. All you see is that upward path in front of you."

"Security, Wanda. It's all about security."

"It's about your childhood, and your fear that you're like your father."

John stiffened, his jaw muscle twitching. Then with a snort, he tossed his head to one side. Wanda sensed that with the gesture, he also tossed his emotions away like yesterday's bathwater. His face relaxed, but a muddy cloud still covered his eyes when he responded.

"My father was a longhaired, guitar-strumming fool in a psychedelic van. He drove in one day, got an oil change and left a tip—me. I never knew the man."

"And you'll never be anything like him. But you're closing in on *my* father, and that's what scares me."

She felt the sting in her throat, the pressure behind her eyes. Tears were coming, and she couldn't stop them. She turned her head away. She didn't want to cry.

For once *she* wanted to be logical and contained. If she managed that, maybe he would listen. He would certainly tune her out if she became emotional, but she couldn't keep from crying. The first tear fell....

He raised her chin. She kept her eyes downcast, but when he brushed the curls from her face and kissed her lids, she looked up.

His eyes were soft as though trying to absorb her tears. *He was trying to understand. He was.*

"Your father did the proper thing. He worked hard, supported his family."

"He abandoned us," she said, shaking her head.

"He died. You want to get picky over definition, fine, but most people wouldn't use the two terms interchangeably."

"Work obsessed him just like it does you. My father left us long before he died, and you're stuck in the same rut. Get out before it's too late."

She paused, breathless, exhausted. Her heart pounded in her throat, threatening to strangle her as she waited for him to finally acknowledge that he understood.

But John cocked his head and stretched his lips in a grimace.

"Wanda...you're exaggerating," he said.

A phantom punch slammed into her diaphragm. Air whooshed from her lungs. She felt numb, as numb as an anesthetized patient awaiting major surgery—heart surgery.

She was wrong. He didn't understand. How could he not? Was she already too late? No. She refused to accept that. A glitch—she was only experiencing a temporary setback. She'd dealt with those before. With a little creative thinking, she would have things back on track.

Wanda wiped the tears away with the back of her hand. She squared her shoulders, pushed her emotions off stage, and marched off toward a far clump of trees.

"This isn't the way we came." John rushed to her side and kept time with her step. "This path is barely visible."

"It's a shortcut."

"Are you sure? Looks like it hasn't been used in years."

"Don't give me any of your cracks about my sense of direction. I know where I'm going. Dusty and I always used this path when we were kids."

"Precisely. Hasn't been used in years."

His sarcastic comment clawed at her, but she didn't answer back. After all, he was still following her. If he wanted, he could have struck off on his own.

Twenty minutes later, they were deeper in the park, standing at the edge of an unkempt lily pond with no exit in sight. Had the gate been moved? She had no clue, but she'd be darned if she'd admit that. Nor would she turn back and confirm her poor sense of direction. Nothing to do, she decided, but charge forward. Sooner or later, some landmark would jar her memory.

She stepped closer to the brackish mire. Reeds, jutting out of the water, clustered in an overgrown clump toward the far side of the stagnant water. A path of stones snaked through the floating plants. They would have to cross on those stones, but that wasn't the only drawback. The smothering odor of decaying greenery took that honor.

She looked left, then right. She knew this area, but it looked both familiar and strange. Such an odd feeling, like trying to recall the lyrics of a favorite tune, knowing no matter how hard she strained now, she wouldn't remember until two o'clock in the morning.

But I need to know now. She was ready to give up when she remembered.

"There used to be a little bridge connecting these ponds," she said. "Once we cross over, we'll be able to see the exit."

Algae covered the stones, making them dark and slippery. She picked her way across, occasionally wobbling, but maintaining her balance. She held her breath, and didn't inhale until she reached the grassy spot.

Unfortunately, her relief proved temporary. Tiny green leaves littered the area before her, but underneath she could see patches of root beer colored water. It was a swamp!

"You're lost," he whispered.

She felt his warm breath on her neck and shivered. Why was he so close? Did he want her to tumble into that murky mess? She swayed, then stood erect, determined that if she went, so would he.

"Don't worry. I picked up a park map at the entry gate," he said, unfolding the map he retrieved from his back pocket. "According to this, the exit is due East. Thataway." He pointed his finger across her nose.

"You've had that thing all day? And you let me tramp around here for hours going in the wrong direction?"

"You insisted. Whether we hiked for hours, I couldn't say. No watch, remember."

"Aaahh!" She felt like throwing something: a plate—no, a platter. She had neither, so she made the hardest fist she could and swung.

John veered to the left just as she wound back. Unfortunately, he veered too far. He waved his arms, beating the air, grabbing for support that didn't exist. She saw his foot slip, saw him fall backward in slow motion, and closed her eyes just before he splashed into the water.

The vegetation made his collision sound like a

heavy stone falling into mud. She opened her eyes, expecting to find him swallowed up. He wasn't. He sat, knees bent, arms spread for support. Green and brown goop surrounded him, eased down his pants legs, and spotted his face.

"Is it deep?" she asked.

He didn't answer, just sneered, tried to stand and fell back in.

"Shall I give you a hand?" She reached down to offer help.

"I'd like nothing better," he said through clenched teeth.

The look in his eyes stopped her. They narrowed to slits, the kind of slits you would spy peeking from the crevice of a rock.

"On second thought..." she said, crossing back over the stones as quickly as she could.

She kept her back to him and her head down, not wanting him to see how much his accident had shaken her. When John approached, she turned toward him, collected and ready to apologize, but he strode past her.

"Let's go," he said, not missing a beat.

"No. You're angry; I'm not going anywhere with you if you're angry."

John stopped and faced her, his mouth stretched into a ventriloquist's smile.

"I'm not angry. I'm cold and wet," he said through his teeth.

"See, you're angry."

"Fine. Stay here, but I'm leaving. If you change your mind, I'll drop you off at Dusty's after I stop by my motel."

He started up a rise. She watched, then scurried after him. "Why not drop me off first?"

"Because my motel is close by."

"You can't be serious. The only motels around here rent by the hour."

"I hadn't planned on staying long. This dating business took me by surprise."

"Oh, I'm sure it did. You expected to come down here, throw me kicking and screaming over your shoulder, and drive right back to D.C."

"More or less."

She halted. "More or less what?" she asked, hands on her hips.

"Less the kicking and screaming part," he said as he continued up the hill.

"I wouldn't dare leave that out," she shouted, feeling a good kick to his shin was in order. He had no idea what was at stake if he thought going through the motions of dating would placate her. By the choice of his lodgings, he'd obviously calculated that pacifying her would take less than twenty-four hours.

The hill proved steeper than it appeared. By the time they reached the crest, her face felt hot and prickly. Her leg hurt where the basket swung against it, and her arm ached from carrying the awkward thing. She didn't mind; the hike had provided one blessing. It seemed to have extinguished John's anger.

What stood in its place, she couldn't say. She looked up into his face, unable to read his emotions clearly. He was frowning; no, he was smiling—barely, and he was standing with his arms folded across his chest. He looked ready to lecture.

She couldn't bear that any more than she could

endure another argument. And her plan—it didn't stand a chance if they argued away every date.

Tension polluted the air. The only freshener capable of clearing it away was an apology, and just looking at John's rigid stance, she knew it wouldn't come from his lips.

She took a deep breath and began.

"I'm sorry," she said.

"You've been saying that a lot lately."

"What..."

"Listen, sweetheart, I can't stand here and argue. If I stay in this wet goo much longer, I'll sprout vegetation. So what would you prefer, a mutant or me?"

"Is that a trick question?"

He inhaled one long breath.

"Okay, your motel, but no funny stuff."

He spread his arms, the picture of innocence. "Straitlaced, boring guy that I am—how could you think it?"

Just then, the wind picked up, blowing a few fallen leaves around them. She gasped in surprise at its force as twigs and dirt scratched at her legs. John buried her face in his chest, protecting her from the flying fragments. His heartbeat boomed in her ears.

His warmth enveloped her, infusing her with a strong desire. She snuggled in, knowing her action would probably send him the wrong message, but she couldn't separate herself from his embrace, from this man she longed to return home with. Back home.

The wind stirred again, sending a whiff of algae her way, bringing her back to reality.

Not yet, she thought, and pulled away. She still had a task ahead of her. She wouldn't be derailed. The realization of how easily that could happen, and that

John lay ready to take advantage of her weakness, rekindled her anger. She looked up, prepared to call off the trip to his motel, but he spoke before her.

"That little whirlwind is nothing compared to Tornado Wanda," he said, his eyes sparkling behind his glasses. His lips slanted just enough to nick a dimple in his right cheek.

His smile was like a pin piercing her hot balloon, letting all her anger escape. She closed her eyes, slowly exhaled and felt the tightness in her chest ease.

"Is that how you see me?" she asked, gazing up at him. "Unpredictable and destructive?"

"Unpredictable, yes," he said picking leaves from her tangled curls.

"Destructive?"

"Depends. Are we counting this picnic?" His smile broadened.

"I prefer we didn't, but you must admit, it was different." She surprised herself with a small laugh.

"Food went everywhere...except my stomach."

"Are you saying you're hungry?"

"Nah. Ignore those grinding noises. My stomach does that every six hours or so," he said. He took her elbow, and steered her toward the gate. "Come on, we'll grab a bite somewhere, but first, my motel. While I change, you can check out the Jackson designs I brought down with me."

His lips twisted into a sly grin. She smiled back cautiously. Why was he inviting her to look at his work? He hadn't done that in years.

Don't be so suspicious, she told herself. This was one change she should welcome. Perhaps her plan was working, glitches and all.

She passed the basket to him. "Lead on," she said, still unable to shake the feeling she'd just been invited up to his room to see his etchings.

5

AT LAST, WANDA WAS in his hotel room. True, not under the conditions he had hoped—with champagne chilled and waiting after their five-course dinner—but he could take it from here. He was good at ad-libbing. Wanda had underestimated his resourcefulness. He could handle the impromptu, especially when he had been given enough time to prepare. Fortunately, he'd had all morning arranging this little coup.

Actually, she wasn't in his room just yet. She stood poised in the hallway, staring inside, as if debating whether to cross the threshold.

"I'll gladly carry you over," he said.

She rolled her eyes and entered. "This certainly isn't your usual pay-by-the-hour establishment," she said, surveying the room.

"Try pay-through-the-nose." He followed behind while she ventured into the sitting area of his suite.

"I'll say," she agreed. "Plush carpets, high ceilings, nice artwork..."

He watched as she examined the Monet reproduction hanging over the mahogany side table. She touched the porcelain vase and sniffed the fresh flowers it held.

"This is one of the most expensive hotels in the city," she said.

"Spice doesn't come cheap."

"This isn't like you at all. I mean, spending this kind of money on something so unrelated to work."

He smiled to himself. *Wrong.* In reality, this was work-related. He couldn't fully concentrate on his designs until he'd rendered her spice-sated and homeward bound. If he played this right, he could have his life back to normal by the end of the evening. They could check out in the morning and drive back to D.C. After dropping her off at home, he would head for the office. If they left by seven, he'd be at his desk no later than ten. That would give him all day to work on the Jackson designs and give Wanda all day to put the house back in order.

But he had to play it right...no rushing and certainly no pouncing like the other night. Slow, smooth and irresistible. He followed her across the room and stood behind her as she moved toward the large double doors.

"What's in here?" she asked, swinging them open to reveal a king-size bed covered with an ivory cutwork comforter.

"Oh," she gasped, and bumped into him in her haste to escape.

"Standard hotel equipment, just bigger than most. Like to try it?"

"I thought we came here so you could change your clothes and I could see your drawings." She slipped by him, grazing his body with her own.

Long after that incidental caress, his skin continued tingling. He drew in his breath, held it and waited for his muscles to relax. When they didn't, he chanted to himself, "Slowly...move slowly."

Finally, he regained control, but the aftereffect left him feeling light-headed, lost. He couldn't take much more of this torture. He needed either to get her home soon or get himself to an asylum.

"So, where are the sketches?" she asked.

"Over there." He pointed to the oval table by the sliding patio doors, and escaped into the bedroom.

He turned on the shower, full force and cold. He had more than mud to battle.

When he reemerged, clean, damp and still bothered, he discovered Wanda bent over the drawings, elbows resting on the table, head cradled in her hands, and her hips swinging to whatever tune she quietly hummed. A ballad, he decided. She moved much too slowly for rock 'n' roll.

Desire zipped through him as he watched her slow drag. He imagined his hands around her full hips, pulling them to him, molding them into the hollow of his lap.

His heart beat faster and his blood drained from his extremities to pool in his center. He closed his eyes, trying to block the sight of her, but her whispered song echoed in his head, and behind his closed eyes he saw Wanda and their house and their empty bed. He would be anything she wanted, if only he knew what that thing was.

Unfortunately, he suspected Wanda didn't know, either. Spice and whimsy couldn't cause this much angst. Something else festered at the core of her unrest. The baby syndrome, perhaps? He hoped not.

Then, from some dark corner of his mind, a thought bushwhacked him, slamming into his chest with breath-robbing force. Could she have fallen out of love with him and not know it?

His eyelids shot open, but the shock of the idea locked all his other muscles in place. Sweat speckled his forehead as he stood stiff-limbed, looking at her. She danced on. Yes, he would be anything she wanted just to join her right now. He would even fake it. Anything, he decided; he would do anything to keep her love.

Then, as if teasing him, she paused in midswing, lifted her curls off her neck, and sifted them through her fingers. They tumbled back, slow-motion, into place.

He exhaled and turned away. The urge to rush over and wrap her in his arms had reached pressure point. If he didn't act now, he would erupt.

Hey, Rocko. Down boy. This here situation calls for a touch of the old savoir-faire. You'll lose her for sure, acting like a caveman packing a club. Let your charm tiptoe up on her and drive her wild with desire. Then you can hit her over the head and drag her home.

"Thanks for the advice," he said aloud, startling himself from his daydream.

"I haven't given any advice yet." She turned, head cocked and fingers still combing her hair. "Are you hinting I'm taking too long?"

"Take your time. In fact, take a seat. Please." He pulled the chair out for her. When she moved for the seat, he turned gesturing to the sofa. "On second thought," he said, moving away with the chair in tow, "take a break."

The thump of Wanda hitting the floor spun him around.

Her eyes expanded to twice their normal size; her cheeks glowed a deeper rouge. Her hair fell in her face and she blew at a stubborn curl with no result. The fall had twisted her jersey and hiked it up, exposing her belly. Right then, she looked about the best thing he'd even seen on two legs...or butt.

"Lunch breaks, coffee breaks...those I understand. Tailbone breaks, I can do without," she said, shifting to one hip and rubbing her backside. "Promise me you don't have an encore?"

She moved to her knees, but before she got any farther, he swooped her up, wrapped her in his arms, and molded her to his chest. They stood nose to nose, lips practically touching without him having to lower his head. He had literally swept her off her feet.

"So you *do* perform an encore." Her voice sounded strained, choked. "You're squeezing the life out of me."

"Oh," he said, and released her so abruptly, she staggered backward. "Here, sit." He maneuvered her to the sofa and plopped her onto it. No commendations for suavity thus far. Maybe he should consider the caveman method.

Wanda sat erect, thumping her chest with every exaggerated breath.

"At least I can still give you palpitations," he said.

"They're not palpitations. I'm trying to breathe."

"Sure," he said, crossing to the small refrigerator. She still loved him, but for good measure, he would make sure this night's lovemaking reinforced her affections. By the time he'd finished pouring two glasses of champagne, his panic had evaporated.

He turned to the sofa. Wanda wasn't there. She was at the table, not swinging her hips, but sitting straight and businesslike in one of the chairs. In three strides he crossed to her and stood, offering the wine and smiling at her frown.

"Champagne?" she said.

"Comes with the room," he lied. "No sense wasting it."

She placed the glass on the table without taking a sip, and refocused on the drawings.

He moved closer to her. Too close. Even though it mixed with the scent of potato salad, he could still discern the lemon splash she used after baths. He closed his eyes and imagined her stepping from the shower. The thought of water beading down her body, slipping into places he longed to touch, made his heart thrash. It pounded against his ribs as if trying to rip free from his chest. His pulse answered his heartbeat, and echoed in his head with a volume so loud it pushed him to the edge of deafness.

He gripped her chair, relieved that his bulge pressed into the cushions and not her back. Again, he ordered his body under control, this time by holding his breath and counting to ten. Twenty. Thirty. Not an easy matter. By the time he reached forty-eight, he gave up trying.

He looked down at the top of her head. If she was having similar feelings, she hid them well. Maybe she *didn't* love him any longer.

Of course she does. Come on, Rocko. Make a move. At this rate, it'll be New Year's before you unwrap the present.

I thought you said don't pounce.

Yeah, but you better do something before she gives you the auld lang syne.

"I see something," she said, giving him an excuse to lean closer.

Now, with one hand on the back of the chair, the other on the table inches from hers, he enclosed her in a semiembrace. His face grazed her hair. The catch he heard in her breath encouraged him.

"So do I," he said.

She set the drawings side by side and pointed to the first. "This one dated four days ago...it's basically the same design you did here." She pointed to the last sketch in the queue. "And you did that one three months ago. I thought you made changes."

"Mmm-hmm." He blew in her ear now, and twisted one of her curls around his finger. "I made so many changes I'm back where I started," he answered, nuzzling her mane. "Think circular."

"My guess is you were thinking square." She pushed her hair behind her ear, bopping his nose in the process.

John straightened, grabbed his champagne and chugged. They were rocking off track. He hovered between panic and passion, pouncing and retreating. He had gotten her to his hotel suite all right, but she remained one room's distance from his bed. And he remained one love scene away from resolving this issue.

What made him suggest she look over his designs, anyway? He knew she would only start criticizing. She was already attacking his life-style and his character. Why invite her to assault him on all fronts?

"So, why are you trying to bag this account?" she asked.

"It's big. Very big. R and S can use that type of feather in our caps. Besides, it's good practice." John lowered his voice to a soft jazzy bass, and traced Wanda's ear with his little finger. "He's not the only difficult character I have to deal with right now."

Again she pushed her hair away, but this time John moved quickly enough to avoid her hand.

"If you get this account, then what?" she asked.

"What do you mean, 'then what?' Then we're in contention for all the big jobs."

"And...? You're in contention for the big contracts. So?"

"I don't understand you." Nor did he get the feeling he'd ever regain control of this conversation.

"But I understand you, John Rockman. It's exactly what I told you in the park—you're letting your childhood fears rule you. We're not poor. We have more than we need, and R and S is already one of the best small firms around. Why spoil it?"

He cocked a wry grin and pushed the words out the side of his mouth with a lightness he didn't feel. "Insurance, sweetheart. When the market crashes like it did back in '29, Old Rocko ain't going to be caught short."

He suspected she hadn't heard a word he'd spoken. She sat on her charger, bearing down for the kill. Thank goodness no plates laid around for her to throw. Her champagne flute was the only hurl-worthy object, and she seemed very reluctant to touch it.

"So you secure a few wealthy clients and that opens the door for a parade of bigwigs wanting buildings," she continued. "But that won't be enough—you'll want them all. You won't be happy until you become king of the hill. Numero Uno."

"I don't see what's wrong with that," he said through his tightening throat.

"Suddenly you'll get so big, you and Larry will have trouble handling all the business yourselves.

You'll hire junior architects to do the creative work, and what will you be left with?''

"More time with my wife. And family," he added—an afterthought, but one he hoped would diffuse her energy. It didn't.

"Bull! You'll have the nuts and bolts—the administrative stuff. The contract negotiations, site inspections, the clients to wine and dine. All the politicking!''

"Nonsense.'' He didn't want to hear the truth in what she said, but he couldn't block it out.

"It's the creative work you like, but the only time you'll be putting pen to paper would be to sign someone's paycheck. Do you really want that?''

"I'm missing your point,'' he said.

So, he would have to delegate some of the design work. Success carried a price. He could live with the change. Besides, he wasn't getting much satisfaction from the actual design work anymore, thanks to Jackson. Giving that part up altogether posed no problem; in fact, it would solve some. He could live without the creative aspect, he told himself. Sure he could, if Wanda would only ease up.

"Just like a dame,'' he said, letting Rocko take over. "A fella gets his foot on the ladder, ready to rise, and bang. She shoots him down. Relax—don't frizz your perm. None of these big changes will come down unless Jackson is taken care of.''

She blinked twice. Her eyes turned a cloudy turquoise. John waited, hoping this time his sudden character change would divert her attention. His Hollywood takeoffs could disarm her blackest moods and her most entrenched position. But that hadn't happened in years.

How could he make her understand? He valued structure. It had gotten him where he was today, almost thirty-five and about to become one of the top architects in the country. He couldn't have achieved that functioning on impulse. Such achievements took discipline.

And sacrifice.

Yes, that too, but he was determined not to sacrifice Wanda or his marriage. Somehow, he would show her the logic behind his approach to life, and end this spice-and-spontaneity kick of hers.

And the sooner the better. Sunday was almost over. He would be back in the office on Monday, and still needing to finalize the plans for Jackson's new building. He didn't have time for long-distance dating.

"So, what do you say, babe? You got this Jackson character figured, or what?"

She stared at him, her brows drawn tight enough to pass for thatched overhangs.

"Pull up a chair," she answered at last. "I have a few suggestions, and afterward, you can take me straight to Dusty's. Forget about going out to eat. Between you, Jackson and Rocko I've developed one heck of a headache."

There goes our evening of passion, he thought, taking a seat and inching closer to her. "Shoot," he said, but the look Wanda gave him warned he'd best rephrase that direction.

"Let's hear your suggestions." As he moved a safer distance away, he wondered how much of his plan could be salvaged.

The bud of an idea sprouted. He twisted and turned it, testing its feasibility. Finally he grinned, pleased with the plan's simplicity.

Why hadn't he thought of it sooner? Now he would have to wait until next weekend. In the meantime, he would give Wanda a little something to worry about. A little something to keep her so occupied, she wouldn't have time to develop any schemes of her own.

6

THE MINUTE WANDA STEPPED into Dusty's living room, with her hair bound in a bath towel, her sister's short terry robe wrapped around her and John giving her the once-over, she knew she had made a mistake.

Why had she let him talk her into eating over here? She inched backward, ready to flee to her bedroom and lock the door if he made the slightest move toward her. But when he strode forward, she froze. Just anticipating his touch, she needed to shower all over again.

"I'm starving," he announced, walking past her and turning into the kitchen. He opened the refrigerator.

"Not much in there," she said to his hunched back.

"There's enough for an omelet. You get dressed while I take charge in here."

"Sure. I'll just be a minute."

She backed out of the room feeling anything but sure. Why should she feel rejected because he chose the refrigerator over her?

"Wait, aren't you going to quiz me?"

"What?" She stopped outside the bedroom door and stared at him bathed in the yellow light of the fridge, his hands covering his eyes.

"Go ahead, ask me what you have on," he said.

"Don't be silly."

"What's wrong, afraid I'll get it right?"

"O.K. What do I have on?"

"Under that skimpy robe...nothing."

Any fool could be as accurate, but still she felt heat steal up her neck. Fortunately, John's hands still covered his eyes; he missed her blush. But heat wasn't all she felt. Cool air crawled under the hem of the robe, and caressed her damp thighs. Nothing was all too correct.

"I—I'll only be a s-second," she stammered and escaped into the bedroom.

She took ten minutes, but when she joined him in the kitchen, she felt calm and protected in her uniform of frumpy blue sweats. All the same, she maintained a safe distance while the two of them bumped about the kitchen.

The space was too small to eliminate contact. Each time they brushed, her skin contracted and her stomach somersaulted. By the way he jumped whenever she neared, she suspected he was experiencing similar reactions.

Finally, she stepped aside and gave him room. John moved around with the precision of a master chef. She loved watching him create in the kitchen. She could think of nothing sexier than following his smooth movements as he prepared a meal especially for her.

He wielded the cleaver as if it were an extension of his hand. Mushrooms, he sliced paper-thin; the ham, he diced and the onion, he reduced to a minced tear factory.

The latter, he sautéed in butter, adding just a pinch of garlic before removing the mixture from the pan. The aroma whiffed around her nostrils and she inhaled deeply. Intoxicating. Her stomach rumbled in response.

When he reached over her for a bowl, she noticed the same smell clung to his clothes. Again she breathed deeply, collecting the scent—a tantalizing combination of food and something distinctly John. Yes, intoxicating.

He went about his task, occasionally flashing her a smile or offering her a tidbit. Finally, using one hand, he cracked the eggs, whisked them to a near froth, and poured them into the same pan. At just the right moment, he added the filling. She closed her eyes and swallowed.

When he slipped the omelets onto the preheated plates and they sat down across from each other, she was hungry for more than food. She kept her attention on her meal and her mind on her no-touch rule.

They devoured the food in silence, then moved to the living room to finish the wine. She had consumed more than her two-drink limit and now her head buzzed pleasantly and her muscles relaxed into the deep cushions as she curled in the corner of the love seat. John sat next to her, refilling her glass. He clinked his goblet against hers, and watched her as she sipped.

The telephone rang, giving Wanda a start. It rang again, the glass coffee table amplifying the sound to alarm-clock shrillness. She lifted the receiver on the third ring and dropped it back onto its cradle.

"That could have been an important call for Dusty," John said.

"She's not here," Wanda said, raising the drink to her mouth.

He raised his brow, set his wineglass down and

leaned back, examining her. Wanda gave a hasty smile, but kept her goblet to her lips even though she had stopped drinking.

She looked into his limpid eyes and felt her heart flip-flop. His gaze captured her, pulled her in and washed her with desire.

The glass clanked against her teeth. She blinked and sat upright. Something too expectant lurked behind his expression. His glasses, she thought. When did he take off his glasses? No doubt about it; he had fallen back into a seduction mode and was moving in for the kill. She braced herself.

"Well, Wanda," he said, leaning toward her. "Thanks for an interesting day, but I must be leaving."

"What?"

"It's late. I have to be in the office early tomorrow." He placed his hands on his knees and stood.

"Oh, I thought—" She stopped herself.

"You thought I was going to make love to you?"

"Yes. No. I mean…"

"Glad I'm not the only one confused by this arrangement of yours."

He hovered over her. She hated when he did that. It never failed to make her feel petite, which for her translated to insignificant. She sprung to her feet, her head ringing from the sudden movement.

"I'm not confused, and you can't say it wasn't on your mind," she said. "Sitting there giving me those bedroom eyes. You even took off your glasses to enhance the effect."

"I took off my glasses to wash my eyes. I chopped the onions for the omelet, remember. So don't flatter yourself, I have no intention of seducing you, not that

it wouldn't be easy to do. You were sitting there panting and puffing louder than an overheated steam engine.

"An overheated steam engine!"

"That's right. Making love to you is the last thing
on my mind, but you must admit, when a man can't
kiss his own wife without suffering backlash and being branded a seducer, something's very, very
wrong."

Wanda stared at him with her mouth open. It was
bad enough she'd read his signals wrong, but he de-
nied even being interested. She continued staring as
he walked into the kitchen and returned with his
glasses.

"I can see now," he said, pushing them in place
with his thumb, "but the picture is no clearer."

"You can't say that's not what you've been up to.
That's how you always win arguments."

"I don't argue. I have rational discussions, but with
you, that's impossible."

"You're impossible. Having a real date with you
is impossible. You spend the day complaining, then
you insult me for seeing through your Don Juan
scheme. I'm so mad—"

"You're mad? I'm the one being criticized. Like
you're perfect."

"I didn't say I was perfect."

"Damn right, you're not. You're unorganized,
rash, immature, and crazy. And you're driving me
crazy trying to read your mind. Well, you know what?
I don't even think *you* know what you want." He
jabbed the air with his finger, then stopped and took
a breath. "I'm going home," he said, running his
hand through his hair. "I'm going to forget this week-

end. I'm going to get a good night's sleep and on Monday I'm going to show Jackson the new designs and hope *he* can make up his mind. You see, Wanda, I can only deal with one crazy at a time.''

"And you prefer Jackson?"

"He's the least complicated." He turned and made for the hall. "Where's my coat?"

"I'll have you know I'm not crazy. I know exactly what I want."

"So do I...my coat," he said, rifling through the closet.

Wanda stomped over and pulled his coat from a hanger.

"One conservative blue sport coat," she said, shoving it into his chest. "The only straitjacket in the closet."

John adjusted the collar, the lapels, aligned his tie, and frowned down at her.

"I told you what I want," she said. "Our lives less regimented, and a lot less rigid. I want you to loosen up, break out of that mold and stop putting our lives on hold."

"That's all?"

"I want you...I want a family."

"And a dog."

"Forget the dog!"

"Gladly. Forget the dog...just the family."

She nodded.

"Fine. We'll go home and start working on it."

She shook her head. "I don't want a family until I'm sure you're ready."

"I'm ready when everything else is in place."

"When's that? After you've cornered the market? That's become more important than *us*."

"No. It hasn't."

"That's what you have to prove."

He moved closer, held her face between his hands and closed his eyes. When he leaned forward, his lips moving to meet hers, she shot her hand over her mouth, intercepting his kiss. His eyes opened wide, and he stared at her long and hard before he straightened.

"That only proves you know how to kiss, which was never up for debate."

"Thanks for keeping something off your list of complaints."

"In spite of it all, you're perfect at lovemaking."

She'd never had reason to complain, yet she couldn't help wondering to what heights they could soar if ever he allowed himself total abandon.

"Now what?" he asked. "You've had your dates...two dates. Spice, as you call it, but if you ask me, it was more like a dose of Tabasco sauce."

"Then you plan one. Just make it something you wouldn't normally do, and make sure it doesn't end with a seduction scene. I need to know you're trying, and I need to know that before even considering going back home. Until then, we date."

"Fine, but you only have four more dates left."

"There you go again. You and your time lines. How do you know four will be enough? You must be open to however many and however long it takes."

"That's where you're wrong, Wanda. I have no intention of dating my wife indefinitely. I've been patient. I've played along—"

"You're right," she interrupted. "That's all you've done—played along. Humored me for a bit and hoped

I would give up. You still don't understand what I'm trying to show you."

"I've been too busy dodging the surprise punches you keep throwing."

"Don't you see? Surprises are gifts. Don't dodge them."

"Yeah, stand there and get flattened. Sounds like a lot of fun."

"No! Don't fight them. Enjoy them, use them. They'll enrich your life. Your designs—"

"My designs? If you're still mad about my late hours, just say so, but leave my work out of it. There's nothing wrong with my designs."

"Your designs used to be full of surprises. They were exciting, they pushed the boundaries."

"And they didn't sell. Now they do."

"Now they're boring."

He glared at her, his eyes dark, almost black. "That does it. I'm leaving."

The hard edge in his voice cut her. She felt her breath seep out, leaving her flat as a punctured tire. She was losing him. He had changed so much from the exuberant young apprentice she'd married.

"I'm going home," he said. "If you're finished with your little adventure, you'll come with me."

Wanda silently mouthed her answer. No. Cold tears blurred her vision, but through them she could see him look at her and slowly, remorsefully shake his head. She blinked and let the first drop trickle down her face. The others followed, one at a time, as if squeezed from a dropper.

"Okay, Wanda. We'll try a few more dates, but I want to leave you with this important thought. I can't live in chaos, so you'd best get over this…this phase. Soon.''

Her eyes dried instantly. *What?* Had he just threatened to end their marriage? The thought roller-coastered through her mind. A sharp, sickening taste invaded her mouth. She wanted to scream. She opened her mouth but no sound came.

''There's one more thing I want to leave you with,'' John said.

With one hand, he grabbed a handful of curls, pulled her head backward and with the other, he clamped her body to his. She gasped and he covered her open mouth with his pressing lips. She couldn't breathe, he was kissing the air from her. She needed to pull free, but she didn't dare part from his demanding kiss.

Without breaking contact, he slowly raised her head and drew her up on tiptoe. Her feet skimmed the floor and then she floated. She threw her arms around his neck. Her kisses matched his. Her tongue met his then entered his mouth with probing, driving, sweeping motions. She kissed him with all the hunger she'd been hiding, trying desperately to burn away all thoughts he may have of leaving her, of leaving their marriage.

John moved to her neck, nibbling, tasting, sucking a pattern from her jaw down to the V of her loose top. Her hardened nipples rubbed against the fleece material. He drew one into his mouth, kissing it through her shirt. His mouth felt hot as a rain forest. His smell, humid and musky, was just as exotic. She shivered and moaned.

He moved away, but then he traced the other side

of her neck, and she tingled with anticipation, knowing his hot mouth would soon claim her other breast.

"Boo!" The loud, playful voice cracked the tension.

Wanda froze.

Dusty. She had forgotten all about Dusty.

"Am I interrupting anything?" Her sister asked, peering around the door at the two of them.

They separated, firewood split apart by the sudden shock of a wedge. The spot where his body had touched hers instantly cooled. She felt abandoned as she watched John straighten and readjust himself.

"Remember," he said and slipped out the door. His voice was hollow, yet final. It echoed in the room and followed him down the hall. His retreating footsteps mimicked the sound of his voice as he descended the stairs. She heard the heavy front doors open and close. After that, all she heard was a frightening silence.

"I did interrupt something? Good. How did you like the 'Boo?' Great touch, huh? And my timing? Perfect. I waited exactly ten minutes after the phone signal, just as we planned. What did you think of my timing?"

"It was lousy," Wanda replied, pulling herself away from the closet and shuffling across the room. She flopped onto the love seat, grabbed a throw pillow, placed it on top of her knees and rested her chin on it.

Suddenly, the crushing weight of failure and loss pushed down on her. Her chest seemed to collapse with a pain she'd never experienced before. The bitter sting of tears attacked her eyes yet again, but this time, they remained dry. She would have gladly surrendered to a deep cleansing cry.

She was lost. She felt hopeless. For once in her life, she had no ideas, no answers. John had said, "or else." There was no doubt in her mind he meant it. What was she to do? She couldn't face living without him. Yet she knew she could not continue living the type of life he had outlined for the two of them.

Wanda released a sigh that sounded to her like the moan of a wounded animal.

"Uh-oh. I smell a glitch," Dusty said, sitting by her side.

"More like a fatal flaw…one that can lose me my husband."

"Which husband? The John you don't want and are trying to change, or the John who hasn't existed in the last few years but you want to resurrect?"

"He thinks I'm going through some crazy phase and he expects me to get over it *soon*."

"So the dating is off?"

"No. He's agreed to one more, at least."

"This doesn't sound promising." Dusty disappeared into the kitchen and returned with a bowl of ice cream.

"Here, the last of the double fudge," she said. "I know your best schemes are chocolate-induced, and from what I'm hearing, you need to rescue your rescue before there's nothing left to save."

"Aren't you having any?" Wanda asked.

"I had my yearly ration the other day. Just watching you, I'll probably gain four more pounds."

Wanda dived into the chocolate mound, filled her spoon, and sucked in its contents, as slowly as if she were eating through a straw.

"Just like him to expect everything to fall into place *soon*. Well, I need longer than that to help a man as haunted by his childhood as John is. That's what this whole workaholic-security thing is all about, you know."

"I figured. Remember Granny's old saying, 'Show me someone with an overstuffed cabinet and I'll show you someone who has survived a famine.'"

Wanda paused, her spoon in midair. "But my someone is so busy collecting food, he doesn't take time to eat. That's going to change," she said and popped the ice cream into her mouth. "I can't stop now."

"Even with his ultimatum?"

Wanda sighed. Either way she'd lose him.

"Even with that," she said, feeling the weight of her words.

"You only have one more date. That's not a lot to work with."

"It's got to pack some powerful medicine, and the one way to do that is to make him desperate for that date."

"Maybe you've had too much chocolate." Dusty reached for the bowl, but Wanda held on tight.

"It's time for stage three. That's when I show him the shadows of things yet to come if he continues living the way he is."

"This has a Dickensian ring, little sister."

"Right. And John is about to get a visit from the most frightening spirit of all."

With a wicked grin spreading on her face, Wanda reached for the phone.

"Who are you calling? John?"

"My boss. Ever since I left, he's been trying to get me back to work."

Dusty sat upright. "But it's eleven o'clock at night!"

"He's an insomniac. If he says anytime, day or night, he means it."

When Wanda hung up, a devilish smile tipped the left corner of her mouth. She tapped the phone against her chin, thinking, and then looked over at Dusty.

"We have a lot of work to do in the next few days."

"We? No...please say you don't mean, *me* we."

Wanda's grin deepened and Dusty groaned.

"I was afraid of that," she said. "I ought to have my head dissected."

7

JOHN SAT AT HIS DESK, staring across to his drawing board, still tasting Wanda's kiss. How long would it take before this silliness of hers played itself out? He couldn't last another week without the touch of her snuggled against him in bed. He surely couldn't last another week of commuting to Richmond and back, not while the Jackson project remained unsettled.

He glanced at his watch. Eight o'clock. The meeting started at ten, which gave him only two hours to review his drawings and anticipate any problems. If Jackson required any more changes, John would write him a bill for the extra paper. "What's our motto?" he asked, and answered himself, "Please the client."

He looked at the boards spread over his desk. A twenty-five story office building with extra amenities to make it "woman-friendly." Jackson, concerned by the high turnover of his skilled female staff, had stressed that.

John failed to see the logic in his client's thinking. While very nice, women's lounges and a rooftop cafeteria wouldn't solve long-standing management issues.

He looked at the drawings again: the sharp angles, the symmetry. Clean, clear, straightforward lines. Boring. That's what Wanda would call it. No surprises, no spice, but Jackson didn't want spice, so

Jackson wouldn't get spice. John knew better than to introduce a bold new image to his already confused client. Wanda liked things guaranteed to shock; he liked things guaranteed to sell.

"Hey, man. You've been staring at those drawings for the past twenty minutes. What are you trying to do? Make them levitate?" Larry leaned against the doorjamb, his hair pulled into a ponytail, his pink, tailored shirt buttoned at the neck and worn without a tie. Red Mickey Mouse suspenders held up purple, loose-legged pants.

John smiled weakly. "If Jackson doesn't like these designs, maybe I will give mysticism a try."

"If he isn't happy this time, I say we build a fire with all the rejects and burn him at the stake," Larry said and chuckled.

John didn't laugh. He looked at the drawings, but his mind wandered.

If they wrapped up the meeting in an hour or less and if the client didn't request any more changes, he could skip out early and drive down to Richmond. He would arrive unannounced, catching Wanda before she had planned any surprises. He would sit her down and the two of them would talk. This thing bothering her had turned his life upside down. He had to straighten it out and get things back to normal. Soon.

"Yo, John. Wherever you are, it's not here." Larry no longer stood in the doorway; he was leaning by the desk waving his palm in John's face. "Snap out of it. Jackson will be here any minute and since I'm the one who gets too excited, you'll have to handle him."

I can handle Jackson, all right, but can I handle Wanda? What would it take to get her back home throwing dishes at his head? No, he could do without her tantrums, but the real question remained. What would it take to become a normal couple again? Was living with Wanda ever normal?

He remembered when they were newly wed, when Wanda still worked, and he and Larry hadn't started their own firm. He'd enjoyed her quirkiness back then. And she hadn't considered him boring, nor their marriage lacking spice.

For the life of him, he couldn't point to the change, at least, not any change in his behavior. He couldn't even remember when the dish tossing had started, or the talk about the dog. Or the baby.

Was that at the heart of all this? Wanda wanting a baby? A dog, he could concede to, but a baby? They couldn't start a family now. They hadn't reached their savings goal, and the firm took up most of his time.

He'd grown up with an absent father, but his child would not suffer the same fate. He would never do that to a child. He wanted his career set, his goals achieved before he would even consider starting a family.

When he and Wanda had first talked about children, they'd agreed to wait. So what had caused her sudden about-face? The answer echoed around him: no job, too much free time.

That made the solution simple. Get her another job. He would start working on that as soon as he finished with the Jackson contract, and as soon as he got her back home.

John smiled. He knew just how to proceed: get wife home, get wife job, get back to normal. But one thing remained crystal clear to him, and he would make

Wanda see it as well. This was no time to start a family.

"We're not ready!" he said.

"What do you mean? Jackson arrives in an hour. What's not ready?"

John snapped to attention. *Get a grip, Rocko, you're talking to yourself.*

"The fire," he said, remembering Larry's comment about burning the client at the stake. "We'll need a permit for an open fire."

"Don't scare me, man. You've been acting so weird since Wanda left, I thought you meant the new designs weren't ready."

"We're as ready as we were last time."

"You sure have a way of instilling confidence. I think I'll go check on that open burning permit."

"Just bring on Mr. Flip-Flop. If he gives us trouble this time, I'll light the match myself."

As JOHN SAT with his partner, watching Jackson mill over the designs, his hopes of driving to Richmond and surprising Wanda idled at the stop sign.

Jackson sat straight-backed in his chair, rubbing his chin as he reviewed the drawing. His ski-sloped forehead and high cheekbones created a canyon that hid his eyes. Jackson's entire face featured so many angles and frown lines, John guessed the man never smiled. Indeed, their client had never done so in his presence. And today, the man looked downright pinched.

Larry paced behind Jackson's chair, making strangling gestures. John sat at the head of the conference table, one hand resting under his chin, the other holding the pencil he'd just used to make more changes.

"Yes…yes, nice." Jackson stared at three drawings, then pushed his chair backward and stood. "But…"

"But what?" Larry squawked.

"But we still seem to be missing the point."

John snapped the pencil in two, placed the pieces on the table, and gestured their client back to the vacated chair.

"Please explain, Mr. Jackson," he said. "Take your time." He kept his face calm, but behind his serene exterior, his spirits turned bluer than the ink on his drawings.

Cancel all thoughts of a surprise trip to Richmond. You aren't going anywhere, Rocko. He settled deeper into his chair.

Four hours later, with his phone calls transferred to Larry's office, John hunched over his desk examining Jackson's rejects. The customer is always right, but what do you do when the customer keeps changing his mind? John answered his own question. You back him into a corner and tell him straight. John lowered his head, squinted and spoke from the left side of his mouth.

"Listen here Jackson, we know what you're up to. You're trying to weasel out, but it ain't going to work, see. We're through playing your games. From now on, it's our ball—what we say goes. You got it?" He pointed his pencil at his invisible guest.

He wished it were that simple. When he'd talked Larry into accepting the challenge, he'd honestly thought it would be simple. After all, Jackson had approached them, not the other way around. For his new office building—The Jackson Towers—he wanted clean, straightforward lines. He wanted fresh talent. He wanted R and S Architects.

Well, he got them all right, and at a bargain, but the prestige of the assignment balanced out the low fee. Now, what originally seemed the opportunity of a lifetime had become a designer's nightmare.

He should have let Larry handle it. What did he have to prove anyway—that he still had what it took, that he could design something other than a box?

John massaged his forehead, trying to rub out the throbbing pain. So far, this contract was only paying off in headaches. He gritted his teeth and erased the columns that, until that morning, had been Jackson's favorite building feature.

John brushed the eraser crumbs away, and stared at the barren spot. Maybe I'll leave it that way, he thought. It fits the clean, straightforward criteria, but he was already at work drawing alternatives to the columnar supports.

Three sheets of paper and one pencil later, he still didn't have the solution. He experimented with size, shape, material, location, but nothing clicked. It would have been far easier if Jackson had stayed to explain himself. Instead, he'd rushed off to his next appointment, leaving John with the feeling of being tumbled and pitched from a clothes dryer: hot, tossed and crumpled.

What did he expect from a high-powered tycoon? From now on, he would limit his clients to nice, re-tired couples living at least five states away and wanting simple log cabins in the mountains.

Knock it off Rocko. You want to be in the big league, see your name in lights. You want to be a contender.

No, no, not anymore I don't. It's too much, I tell you. They're driving me crazy.

So it's getting to you? You're sweating?

That's not all. My hand's shaking. Look, look at my pencil. It's drawing on its own.... I'm not doing it.

Sure you are, Rocko. You want to be Numero Uno. Isn't that what your dame said? You can't stop. You can't help yourself.

Sure I can. I can stop anytime I want. From now on, it's little old ladies and log cabins.

Don't make me laugh. You'll do anything to be on top. Even trade in your marriage.

"No, never," John said aloud in his normal voice and stared across the room seeing nothing.

That's probably what Wanda thinks. I'm doing all this just to be top dog, that it's only for me. But I've explained so many times—it's for us. Once Larry and I are established, our lives will be made. We'll have all the things we need, including time. She can have all the spice she wants...and the dog. And the baby. But she has to wait. Surely that's not asking too much.

He froze in thought, pencil poised in hand, blank paper before him. *Wanda will just have to grow up.* That's all there was to it. He nodded in firm agreement and refocused on the paper.

No design images filled his mind. Instead he saw Wanda, swallowed in one of his shirts and sitting in the middle of their bed. Her wild curls covered most of her face, but not enough to hide her moist, generous lips parting, inviting him to taste.

John closed his eyes and absorbed the picture. He could almost smell her, the clean soapy scent she always had, except after making love. Then she smelled her special blend of musk and heat. His heart pounded and was echoed by another beat, much lower, drumming against the seams of his pants. Shifting in his chair only intensified the rhythm.

Desire roared through his body, pushing away the Jackson headache. His head felt light, as light as a helium balloon. It lifted him up. He was floating, looking down at a smiling, inviting Wanda.

Go for it, Rocko, he thought and dived just as she raised her arm, aimed and threw a plate.

John shot to attention and swerved, pulling his stool off balance. The sound of him crashing to the floor ricocheted off the walls. His long legs intertwined with those of his chair, and every sheet of paper that had been on the desk now covered him.

''You missed,'' he said to the fading image.

"I don't know…looks like a bull's-eye to me." Larry peeked around the doorjamb and scanned the room. "Don't tell me that talking to yourself is not enough? You're taking up self-flagellation too?"

"I fell," John said, kicking his legs free of the chair, then crossing them at the ankles. He folded his arms over his chest. The sound of the paper crackled in his ears.

"Actually, it's not so bad down here. Probably good therapy for my back."

"Huh," Larry snorted. "You plan on staying down there?"

The idea amused John, and he let a big smile serve as his answer.

"My grandmother would have a saying for this. No doubt about it."

"I have my own saying for this."

"Yeah?"

"Yeah. Wanda." John closed his eyes and took a

deep breath. It was Wanda all right. What little bit of his brain Jackson had left intact, she was surely destroying.

"Oh, that reminds me," Larry said. "I came down here to get you. She's here. Wanda is in my office."

8

"YOU WHAT?" John looked at her as though she were speaking in tongues. Then again, to him, maybe she was.

Wanda walked around the oblong conference table, filling time, letting him absorb the information.

"I'm back with my old company, but now I set my own hours," she answered, idly trailing her hand over the chair backs. She was glad to be moving around. Walking helped calm her nerves as well as slow her tongue. If ever she needed to think before diving in, belly first and tongue wagging, now was that time.

And she wouldn't consider sitting, either. No need in giving him the added advantage of towering over her. Even now, standing across the room, he looked down at her.

She consciously maintained a safe distance by staying outside The D.M.S.Z.—The Diminishing Size Zone. Positioning herself anywhere inside that zone meant craning her neck, and holding that pose for any length of time took its toll on her muscles as well as her self-esteem.

"Why?" He finally found his voice, a voice that she noted sounded as flat and strained as a plucked rubber band.

"I thought you'd be happy. After all, it was your

suggestion…my cure, so to speak. You've been harping on it for months.''

"Precisely. So why now?''

She walked to the wall where the Jackson assignment, a series of sketches and blueprints, stretched around the room. Since each drawing was dated, she easily traced the progress or lack of progress.

"How masochistic can you get?'' Wanda asked, shaking her head.

"Sorry?''

She jumped at the sound of John's voice. Had he heard her? Slowly, she turned and scanned his face. He looked more puzzled than angry. No, she decided; he hadn't. *I really must control my tongue.* She started walking again, heading for the windows and the models displayed atop a row of podiums.

"After you left the other night, I started thinking. I want our relationship to change. I want us to have a different, a better life-style, but putting that responsibility all on you is unfair.''

So far so good, she thought. At least she wasn't lying. John stood with his arms folded across his chest, looking too much like a headmaster listening to a student's confession.

"So, you've stopped your spontaneity-and-spice campaign.''

"Oh, no. This is in addition to my campaign. You say I'm rash and immature, and have too much free time. Well, I'm going to work on changing that.''

"Even though you don't necessarily agree.'' John tucked his chin and peered at her.

"Why are you so suspicious? I'm willing to make some changes.'' *Some.* "Maybe we'll both learn something from all this,'' she said.

"This turnaround…it's quite a surprise." His face turned into a checkerboard of contrast, sporting a grin one second, a frown the next.

"But one I thought you would like."

"I do. I do."

He didn't fool her one bit. She could hear the tremor in his voice. Under normal circumstances, he spoke in a smooth, stroking bass. Right now, his voice blared like a poorly tuned trumpet.

"I do," he repeated, nodding his head. "In fact, we'll celebrate. How about lunch? It's just about…" He looked at his watchless wrist and paused. "I'm sure it's lunchtime. Just give me a few minutes to finish up, and we'll leave."

He was almost to the door when she answered, stopping him in his tracks.

"It's three-thirty. I had lunch hours ago. Besides, I've got to get back to work. I'm developing the ad campaign for a new client…under a tight time line, of course."

"Well," he said, running his fingers through his hair. "This calls for a real celebration. Dinner. Someplace fancy…say that new restaurant by the wharf."

"John—"

"I know; it's expensive, but hey, we're on two incomes now. We can afford it. What time do you get off? I'll pick you up and we'll go home together."

"I drove in."

"Oh." Again, he ran his fingers through his hair. "Then I'll meet you back at the house and we'll leave from there."

"From Dusty's? You assumed because I've followed your advice about the job, I would move back, too?"

"Well, yes. You'll be working in D.C. Driving in from Richmond every day is one hell of a commute."

"It's the Nineties. Computers…E-mail. I telecommute. I'm only in the office every other week."

"But—"

"I haven't changed my mind about anything. I'm not moving back until our goals are in sync. The only problem is, I'll be so busy with this assignment, I won't be free for another date for quite some time."

He gawked at her. His arms dropped to his sides. She waited for him to recover with a dry retort, but he didn't. Other than his sharp, irregular breaths, he was silent.

She swallowed hard and felt a stone-size lump pass down and settle in her chest. Seeing him this lost weakened her resolve. She was almost ready to confess—to tell him all about her Scrooge-inspired scheme. Almost.

Where was Rocko when you needed him? Right now she would welcome his wisecracking way of brushing off difficult situations. *Oh, well. It's up to you, sweetheart.*

"Look at the time," she said, displaying her new wristwatch. "Can't be late for my first department meeting."

No longer worried about The D.M.S.Z., she walked toward him and in one smooth maneuver, she tiptoed and brushed her lips across his. Had a cop been present, he would have ticketed her for a moving violation.

"This is actually timed very well," she said when she reached the door. "You're tied up with your Jackson account, and now I have my ad campaign. Who would have guessed our schedules would be the one thing we have in sync?''

With that she walked out and closed the door on a stunned, silent John.

JOHN LOOKED AT his partner and shook his head. ''What's she up to?''

''A full-time job,'' Larry said with a shrug.

''But why, and why now? I've been pushing that agenda for months. She wouldn't budge, now suddenly...boom.'' John rubbed the back of his neck and paced his office. ''No, she's up to something. I know.''

''What?''

''I don't know. Not yet, anyway. First the hoedown, then that mad hatter excuse of a picnic, now this.''

''What's so odd about a job? This one sounds great.''

''Exactly!'' John spun around, his finger in Larry's face. ''It's too good. Too high-powered. Wanda's on this minimizing kick. She wants a career, but only if it's part-time.''

''Smart cookie. Maybe I should go work with her. Or better yet, if you two call it quits, let me know. I could use a wife like Wanda.''

John turned in time to see a blur of green and purple polka dots rush out the door. The trouble was, he could use a wife like Wanda, too. The past few lonely nights had made that painfully clear.

With this job threatening to take up all her time, winning her back would take more work than he had originally calculated. How could she do this?

How could she not? How could she resist tossing

in a surprise wrench or two? She didn't fool him. "Willing to make some changes." Like hell she was. This job thing wasn't serious. He would wait her out; soon she would be announcing her second retirement. He would give her a week.

A week later John sat in his office, watching leaves outside his window caught in a gust whirl helplessly about. He empathized.

"Sure," he spoke into the telephone. "Yeah, business is business. Maybe dinner, then? Oh. No problem."

He dropped the receiver in place and picked up the stack of yellow memos. He selected one, folded the paper in half, in half again and then again until it resembled a square dime. This he flicked into the trash can, selected another memo and repeated the action.

He didn't need to reread them. Their message rang similar to those he'd collected on his answering machine.

Sorry, too busy. Let's reschedule.

When? John wondered. When had become a problem.

"PACK IT UP WITH US, pack it up with us, pack it up with us." Wanda repeated the slogan over and over hoping a corresponding visual would materialize in her subconscious. She twisted a curl around her finger and stared at the blank paper.

Her computer screen displayed a flying vortex. She might as well turn it off. Whenever she got stuck, the only way to work herself out of the slump was with old-fashioned pen and paper.

She picked up her red marker and ran it across the

paper in a sweeping motion. Not quite right, but a start, nonetheless.

"Pack it up with us," she repeated.

"My thoughts exactly," Dusty said. "It's about time *you* packed it up."

Wanda turned to find her sister standing behind her, peeking over her shoulder.

"How long have you been there?" she asked.

"Too long and so have you. Come on, follow your client's advice and pack it up. You missed lunch, you know."

"After all the fudge ice cream I've eaten, I can afford to."

"You missed it yesterday, also…and dinner."

"I'm on a schedule…this has to be ready in three more days."

"Only two weeks on the job and you're sounding more like John than John himself."

"That's the plan, right—a frightening look into the future."

"Well, I'm frightened. Something tells me that your playacting has become reality."

"Don't be silly," she said, wiping ink from her hand. She folded the towel in half, folded it again and again until it resembled a neat square, which she carefully placed in the wastebasket.

"Right," Dusty said, "here, by the way. These just arrived for you." She held up a florist box tied with a large gold ribbon.

"More red roses," Wanda said. "We're running out of room."

"How do you know they're roses?" Dusty asked, removing the ribbon.

Wanda looked around the room and pointed to the five vases, each one overflowing with red roses.

"Actually they're asters and spider mums—purples and blues."

"Really?" She swiveled around to face her sister. "Now we're breaking some patterns," she said, taking the flowers from Dusty and placing them in the vase by her desk.

"And his phone calls weren't? When are you going to break down and go out with the man? This dating thing was your idea, remember."

"Yes, I know, and I will. But I'm on a schedule. He knows we'll go out as soon as I have free time. I've told him that."

"Then you'll appreciate the card he enclosed."

"He sent a card?"

"Yep, 'What are you doing New Year's?' Not too optimistic, is he?"

"I've another big project after this. When I finish…" Wanda stopped. "I guess my scheme has a few unexpected side effects."

"You mean glitches, Ms. Workaholic. And if you don't wake up, the future will be here and gone before you know it."

"Okay. I've learned my lesson, and if this florist shop of an office is any indication, so has John. Next time he calls, I'll—"

"Why don't you call?"

Wanda thought a moment. "Why not, indeed," she said, reaching for the phone.

It rang before her fingers touched it. She looked at Dusty and guessed her own eyes were as wide as her sister's.

9

DUSTY FINISHED zipping Wanda into the spaghetti-strapped dress and stepped back, frowning.

"I don't know about this," Dusty said. "Act three, curtain opens. Scrooge in the graveyard about to come face-to-face with his tragic future. Enter the ghost dressed in a shiny, skintight costume. The mood is all wrong. This won't work."

Wanda pretended she didn't hear. Instead, she twirled in front of the full-length mirror, admiring the gold knit dress. It spilled over her, rippling like liquid, every curve and mound catching the light and throwing it back at her.

"Honestly now, what do you think?" she asked Dusty.

"I think it looks better on you than it ever did on me, which gives me two reasons not to like this plan. Besides, in that outfit, you're shark bait. Your no-touch rule will be about as enforceable as Prohibition. And remember, this time I won't be around to save you."

"That rule is no longer necessary. The guy I spoke to sounded ready to compromise. He's abandoned his seduction scheme."

"Overconfidence has wrecked many an unsinkable ship."

When the bell rang, Wanda glanced at her watch.

"See, he's late. The old John would have been right on time, if not early. He really has changed," she said and shimmered as she flowed toward the door.

WANDA, SITTING PRESSED into the passenger seat, clutched her tiny evening bag so tightly she could feel her fingernails cutting through the cloth.

"All I'm saying is you could have warned me." Her voice sounded sharp, but as far as she was concerned, it wasn't sharp enough.

"But I did. I told you it was a little theater in the country."

He sounded cheerful, not at all defensive. Her obvious anger hadn't affected him in the least. That vexed her even more.

"Little theater in the country doesn't automatically translate into converted barn in a rustic setting with the audience plopped in the middle of a cow pasture."

"I thought you knew. After all, you're the artist...you're the one who keeps up with the cultural scene."

"Well, you should have reminded me." He knew how busy she was with her new job and now another client added to her workload. It was easy to forget some things. A little reminder would have been considerate. She'd done as much for him in the past.

"You saw what I have on. Didn't that give you a clue?"

"I thought you were going back to your hotel to change."

"Go back? I just left the hotel."

She felt her face grow hot. Hadn't she just defended him when Dusty suggested he was a shark?

So why, when he showed up in a sweatshirt and his first pair of jeans in years, had she assumed it was a ploy to maneuver her to his room for champagne and frolic? "You could have warned me," she repeated.

"I wouldn't worry if I were you...you look great in anything you wear. You look absolutely stunning in that dress. I'll be the envy of every man there."

A shock wave rippled through her. *Who is this man I'm sitting beside?* John never gave such blatant compliments. If he ever said anything nice about her appearance, it was in halfhearted agreement to whatever compliment she'd force-fed him.

Any other time she would relish such flattery. Today she could only think of the price she would pay for it. Sitting on the cold, evening-dampened ground in Dusty's too-tight frock and pointy-toed high-heeled pumps smacked of overpaying.

"Who ever heard of outdoor theater this late in the season," she said, hoping he noticed her icy tone.

"Last show of the year. They're just experimenting to see if there's interest. If so, they'll keep it in their schedule."

He looked at her and winked. "Something new. Spice."

Resigning herself to her fate, she sighed and gazed out the window. The sun played peekaboo through the trees. At times it disappeared for long intervals, only to pop out of hiding, having dropped a bit lower into the bottom branches. Soon it would be dark enough for headlights. Why was John on this back road? By the time they got to the theater, all the choice spots would be taken.

"Wouldn't you make better time on the freeway?" she asked.

"I thought since we were early we could take the scenic route. Nice, isn't it?"

"You were late," she said, holding her watch up for him to see.

"Really?" He sounded unconcerned.

"Don't tell me you still haven't fixed your watch." She couldn't believe it. His shrug added to her bafflement. "John, curtain time is six o'clock! How far away are we?"

"There's a turnoff up ahead. It's a shortcut back to the freeway."

"I hope you're right."

He flashed her a toothy smile. "As I remember, you usually complained about me being straitlaced and always correct."

"Today, I'll forgive you."

Thirty minutes later, they were still winding along a narrow country road.

"We're lost, John. Admit it. This road doesn't lead to the highway—it's leading farther into the woods."

"We may get there a little late, but we won't miss much of the play."

"The heck with the play. I don't like these woods and I don't want to spend the whole evening trying to find our way out."

Just then she felt the car lurch and then coast. The silence inside the car came suddenly.

"What's that?" she asked, straining her ears, hoping to hear anything, anything at all.

They drifted along, moving slower and slower until they stopped. She looked outside but could barely make out the landscape. Even the closest trees were mere silhouettes against the deep orange sky.

"We're lost, aren't we? You're stopping because we're lost?"

"We're lost, yes. But I'm stopping because we're out of gas."

"What?" She spun to face him. *Out of gas.* They were in the middle of nowhere. How could they be out of gas?

Her throat contracted. She felt dizzy and nauseous. Her heart thumped violently.

It was dark. They were in the woods, in all likelihood, woods infested with bears and other hungry wild animals. It was too dangerous to walk for help, even if they knew which direction to take.

What would they do? She had to think of something, but she couldn't focus. Panic had clouded her brain.

Then, just as suddenly, her head cleared. They weren't out of gas at all. John always kept an extra can in the trunk, along with his first-aid kit, his spare umbrella and other emergency paraphernalia.

He had planned this. The oldest scheme in the book. Leave it to John to come up with something so unoriginal.

She tried to breathe deeply, but her breath came in short, rapid puffs. A tremor gripped her. She held her hands together to stop their shaking.

How could he? He was still playing along, not taking her seriously at all. He still thought this was a minor disagreement he could win simply by taking her to bed.

She slid sideways, her back resting against the door, and watched him turn the key again and again with the same negative results. How can he look so innocent, she wondered?

She clutched her purse, ready to throw it. No. A kick with her pointy-toed shoe would have more impact, but she decided the car's confined space would restrict her aim. For now, she would play along with his game and see how far he would go to hang himself.

"What about the can of gas in the trunk?" She was amazed how calm she sounded.

"There is no can of gas. Just as there is no umbrella, no flashlight, no box of just-in-case items. I started thinking about how you see me, as so set in my ways. It began to make some sense, so except for the first-aid kit, I got rid of everything. Dumping it felt good, actually. It felt dangerous. But now, I feel like it was the most foolish thing I've done in ages."

"You mean you didn't plan this?"

"Good God, Wanda! We're lost in the middle of the woods. No one will come by and rescue us. Why would I pull such a stunt as that? That's more up your alley, not mine."

"Up my alley? Of all the insulting things to say. I'd never be reckless enough to put our lives in danger. There're wild animals out there. We could be killed—eaten—and no one would know!"

"Calm down. I'm sorry—I didn't mean it like that. We're not going to be eaten. I'll think of something."

"Your phone!" she shouted, suddenly remembering he kept a small mobile with him at all times. She opened the glove compartment and rummaged through it. "Where is it? Did you move it?"

"I got rid of everything except the first-aid kit, remember? The only other things in the car are the blankets and picnic basket I packed for this date."

She stared at him in disbelief. He had nothing. No

gas. No phone. Sure, she thought he was rigid, but she never asked him to become remiss. She slumped down into her seat. Here she was stuck in the middle of nowhere with a reformed Boy Scout.

"Come on," he said, opening the car door. "We can't stay here all night."

He rounded the car and was opening her door before she could react.

"Come on where? I'm not going anywhere. It's getting dark."

"Exactly. It's getting dark, and I suggest we start walking while we can still see where we're going. This is a weekend getaway area. People have little cabins all around here. If we start walking now, we'll happen upon one."

"Or a bear. No thanks. I'm not getting out of this car."

"Okay. Stay here. I'll come back when I find help." He closed the car door and struck off.

Wanda stared after him, watching his back move down the dirt road. Soon he was no more than a silhouette, indistinguishable from the other dark shadows.

The bushes to her left rustled. She looked hard, and saw one large shrub shaking. The wind. But the wind wouldn't rattle only one bush. Suddenly, somewhere to her right, a twig snapped.

"That's no wind," she whispered, ready to flee, but froze, not knowing which was the safest door to open.

The moving bush helped her decide. Shaking violently, its dried leaves sounded an eerie, crackling warning. She threw open the passenger door and sprinted down the path, screaming to John.

She ran, but the tight dress bound her legs, held her back. She grabbed the hem and tugged it up high above midthigh.

Bushes rattled in her wake. Her footsteps slapped the leaf-covered road. She ran on, getting as far as she could from the car and that thing nearby it.

The forest closed around, smothering her in total darkness. She couldn't see a thing. Instinct carried her forward. Instinct and fear.

Then, as though in a bad dream, she heard footsteps. Running steps. They were muffled, distant, but still she could tell they fell much heavier than hers. They surrounded her. They bounced off the trees. Echoing. She stopped and listened, but couldn't tell their direction.

Run, sweetheart. It was Rocko's voice.

Which way...which way? she asked and spun, looking everywhere, checking every bush.

Run!

She followed her own advice and ran. Ran right into a sapling. Its twiggy arms tangled in her hair. She yanked and pulled, suddenly hating the genes that gave her curls.

"Let go!" she screamed, and finally freed herself. She rushed on, ignoring her sore scalp. When she broke the heel of her left pump, she ran on despite the peg-legged feeling.

She could no longer hear the other footsteps. Maybe she had outrun the thing. Maybe her heart was beating so loudly in her ears, it drowned out everything else. In any case, she stopped. She had to stop; she could run no more. Her chest ached. She had to catch her breath.

She bent over, hands resting on knees, and coughed.

"Wanda. Are you all right?"

"Heavens," she screamed, jumping around to face John. "Don't ever scare me like that again." She wheezed and gasped with every other word.

"What are you doing out here? I left you in the car."

"I know where you left me. Back there with that thing."

"What thing? What are you talking about?"

"I've been running for my life...it was chasing me...it was—"

He encircled her with his arms and drew her to him. She gladly let herself relax there, her ear pressed to his chest, his arms, warm and strong around her. He slowly rubbed her back, making shushing sounds as he traced circles between her shoulder blades.

"Calm down."

"But it was chasing me," she insisted. Surely he had heard those footsteps.

"What was chasing you?"

She turned and pointed in the direction from which she'd come. "I don't know what it was. I didn't see it—I just heard it...there, and there, and over..."

The picture came to her all at once, straight out of a low-budget movie. Hysterical starlet running from a nightmare that didn't exist. She broke free of his arms, embarrassed by her own helplessness.

"Never mind," she said, pushing the dress back down to her knees and straightening the hem.

John continued to stare at her, his face skewed by lines of worry. She felt his gaze fixed on her, probing, scanning, looking for signs of injury. Or insanity. She squirmed under his scrutiny, suddenly very conscious of how she must look. Thanks to that tree, her hair was probably reaching for the sky like a frightened hostage. She ran her fingers through the tangles, pulling and twisting what bits she could into a bun.

"I'm fine, really. Stop looking at me like that. Where were you, anyway?"

He thumbed over his shoulder, but kept his focus on her. "I found a cabin just off the road."

"You found help!"

"No. A cabin—it's empty."

She crashed in on herself, suddenly feeling weighted. "Empty? What good does that do us?"

"Shelter. The temperature will drop down below forty tonight. Unless you prefer sleeping in the car, the cabin's a good place to spend the night."

She was just getting over the shock of hearing "spend the night," when she noticed him walking down the road toward the car. She hobbled to catch up.

"You said it's over there. Why are you going back to the car?"

"I may have foolishly gotten rid of my emergency items, but I do have some things that'll come in handy." He opened the trunk and leaned inside.

Wanda moved closer until their sides touched. Her gaze darted about the shadowy woods. Her ears perked, listening for suspicious sounds.

Finally he emerged, pulling an army blanket and a small basket out with him. "Rations," he said.

The mere mention of food made her stomach grumble. She'd skipped lunch, hoping a minifast would help her fit into Dusty's dress. It had worked, but now she was famished. The grumble roared again. She placed her hand over her stomach, in a futile effort to still the noise and suppress the gnawing ache.

"This must be one of those little surprises in life you've been lecturing about," he said. "I suppose I'm forced to be spontaneous now. Well, let's go. The cabin is down the road and over that hill."

This was no little surprise, and if she had her way, it was certainly one surprise she would have gladly dodged. She looked into the dark, in the direction he was pointing, knowing she would see nothing. Then she started walking, but realizing she would make better time in flats, she stopped, broke the heel off the other shoe, took a deep breath and continued following him.

Over a hill. Of course. Yes, this date was turning into one nightmare of an adventure.

The moon rose while they trekked through the woods. It wasn't quite full, but near enough to throw a bright silver-white light over the landscape. The trees weren't as large and thickly bunched as they had first seemed. Above, the lapis blue sky canopied them. An occasional dark cloud broke the symmetry. This place wasn't at all frightening. It was beautiful. She stared, amazed by what a little night light could do.

By the time they reached the clearing, she was breathing heavily. She barely noticed the small cabin drenched in moonlight, until they stood near its wrap-around porch.

"Well, I guess we don't have to knock," she said as she leaned against the railing.

John dropped the rations, walked out into the clearing, and started searching on the ground. "Help me find a good-size rock."

"Why?"

"To break a window. These places are all locked up, closed for the season. I'll break that pane by the knob. Don't worry, I'll leave money and a note. Here's a perfect one," he said, returning to the porch, hefting the stone in his palm.

She stepped between him and the target. "Have you tested it?"

"Who in their right mind would leave a place unlocked in this day and age?"

She slipped her hand around the knob and turned it. The latch clicked; the door swung open. "Just a thought," she said, gesturing for him to enter first.

He stood, his puzzled look fixed on the open entry.

"Don't tell me you're waiting for me to carry you over the threshold?" She stepped over the sill, not waiting for his answer.

Once inside, she noticed the smell. She expected the telltale musk most places developed when they were closed tight and out of use. Instead, she detected the clean odor of fresh paint and polished wood.

She ventured into the middle of the room and was immediately struck by the brightness. The entire back of the house was a two-story wall of glass broken only by a ceiling-to-floor stone fireplace built smack in the middle. A sliding glass door was placed so perfectly in the wall to the left of the fireplace, she hardly noticed it.

Beyond the windows and ribboned by trees, lay a lake—still, and like the glass wall, offering another play surface for the moon rays. A path wound down to a pier where a small boat was tied. Silver light looped all of it into a beautiful package.

A calmness washed over Wanda as she absorbed

the scene. Indeed, a perfect place to be stranded. Still she searched the opposite shore for an electric light or two—anything signaling another cabin and help. She saw nothing.

She turned her attention back inside. Moonlight streamed in, illuminating the white upholstered love seat and chair facing the fireplace. She walked to the sofa, turned around and inspected the rest of the room. A heavy wooden table with four captain's chairs were off to the right with a small, functional kitchen just beyond it. The cabinets lining the kitchen wall were small. When she opened them, a faint scent of shellac floated out. Empty. She couldn't help the sinking feeling that came over her, nor the wave of hunger.

"That's probably the master suite," John said.

She followed his line of focus up the open staircase to a loft.

"And this must be the guest suite." He patted the back of the love seat. "I'm sure there's no electricity, or heat. We're lucky to have this fireplace."

He walked about as he talked, flicking light switches with no results. "Déjà vu," he said with a wry grin, then hit another switch and the porch area lit up.

"Must just be the inside bulbs," he said, poking his head into a little closet of a room and disappearing inside.

In a few seconds, Wanda heard a flush. They may starve tonight, but at least one of their needs would be attended in comfort.

"Can't imagine why they left the water on," he said.

"For the same reason they left the door open—they were expecting us."

John gave a half laugh.

She thought she heard a catch in his voice, but dismissed the notion. After imagining she'd heard a bear, she no longer trusted her ears. John was probably nervous about taking over some stranger's house. God knows she was. But unlike her, he was making the most of their unfortunate circumstances.

She watched him kneeling in front of the fireplace, carefully taking logs from the wood box and laying them out. Skillfully, he placed the smallest logs over bits of kindling, and topped the pile with the larger, slow-burning ones. His actions were as meticulous as ever, but for once, she appreciated that fact. Can't keep a good scout down, she thought.

Soon a fire crackled to life. The room filled with a yellow glow that pushed aside the cool, sharp whiteness of the moon. Everything softened. The shadows grew fuzzy; the furniture edges and even the fireplace stones seemed to round to a touchable smoothness. The love seat became ivory-tinted and welcoming. She moved around and sat on the floor, her back resting against the sofa.

A few feet away from her, John sat on his haunches warming his hands. His dark hair picked up the fire's hues and came alive with red and yellow highlights of its own. She imagined that touching it would be like running her fingers through a crackling electric current. Her palms prickled at the thought. A warm feeling spread over her. She knew it wasn't caused by the fire; John's broad back blocked most of that.

As if summoned by her thoughts, he turned and sat beside her. His body was warm from the fire and his heat passed through her, reaching down and settling deep in her core. She felt helpless, helpless as the

kindling against the spark of his match. He was one
heck of a fireman, one who started, not quenched
flames. And she wasn't sure she wanted this one
doused.

She glanced up at him. Could he sense what she
was feeling? He looked directly into the light, as
though hypnotized.

In the yellow glow, his strong features softened.
His lips, no longer pressed tight in concentration,
were relaxed and full. They eased into a smile that
warmed her more thoroughly than any hearth fire ever
could. They coaxed a smile from her and she looked
up into his eyes, startled to find him watching her.

Suddenly she felt weak. Her insides became a jig-
gling mass of gelatin.

Slowly, the resentment she was feeling for an evening gone bad melted away.

10

HE DIDN'T KNOW which made him hotter, the fire or Wanda. He chose Wanda. A few blazing logs couldn't cause a burning this deep, this acute.

So far, he'd maintained control. He didn't know how long he could last, however. Not with the way she kept looking at him, her lids half-closed over smoky eyes—eyes that hinted of something exciting smoldering deep within. It took every bit of his waning willpower to keep his hands on his knees and not on her.

She was staring at him, he could tell, but he kept his focus on the fire. The longer he avoided looking at her, the longer he could avoid pouncing. Even though it would qualify as a spontaneous act, pouncing would not win him points.

He needed a distraction, something to keep his mind off Wanda and this perfect setup. He remembered the basket of food and jumped to his feet.

"We have a fire going, but it won't keep us warm unless we take care of our stomachs."

"What?"

"Didn't you know your body temperature drops when you're hungry? You diet all the time. Don't tell me you've never noticed?"

Boy, he wished he could stop babbling. She eyed

him as though he were an alien. Whatever had smoldered behind her eyes earlier was now extinguished.

"And after our stomachs?" she asked.

"Bed. The one up in the loft is probably roomy, but also cold. We'll stay by the fire." He patted the love seat. "This looks like a sleeper. Small, but it'll make a good bed for us."

That was the second time he'd implied they'd be sharing a bed. If he was lucky, she hadn't noticed.

"*Our* bed? You assume we're sleeping together?"

Damn. She noticed. "It's warmer that way. The temperature's supposed to drop—"

"Yeah, yeah. Below forty."

"Thirty. Into the thirties."

She tilted her head and regarded him. He didn't know what to make of her expression. It wasn't anger. He could definitely rule out delight. No, she wore one of her what's-next looks. The kind she gave him whenever he came home late and she either didn't believe, or was bored by his excuse.

He watched the corners of her mouth turn up. No, she didn't look bored. She just wasn't buying his weather report. *At least she's smiling.* With a little food in her stomach...who knows?

Taking the basket in one hand and the blanket in the other, he crossed to where she sat. He unfolded the cover, spread it before the fire, and placed the bounty on top.

It wasn't an abundant feast—two bottles of wine, grapes, cheese, and two loaves of French bread—but he'd remembered everything, even extra large dinner napkins, a candle and holder, real wineglasses and china plates, though he felt uneasy about the last two items. If she got upset, she now had ammunition. He would just do his best not to irritate her. Not to that extent, at least.

"As organized as ever, I see." She said it with a smile.

"I have your picnic to live up to. Besides, I thought it would be a nice touch. At the play...sitting in the grass, that is." How tongue-tied could he get, he wondered as he uncorked the red wine and filled both glasses.

"Yes, a nice touch," she said, looking over the top of her goblet.

The red liquor grabbed the light and reflected a crimson blush across her face. He leaned over to touch his glass to hers.

"Here's to those little surprises you speak so highly of. Enjoy."

Just as the goblets met, wind rattled the windows and came howling down through the chimney. The flames flattened against the charred logs, then flickered back to life. She shivered and seemed to draw inside herself, her eyes growing large as she stared at the wall of glass.

The clouds had thickened and now hid the moon. The outdoor spotlights lit the porch area, but beyond that lay blackness.

Snow started falling. He could see the flakes drift in and out of the porch light. At first, it came softly, slowly, but in no time it erupted into a whirling madness. He saw Wanda pull up to a rigid alertness.

"Oh, no. How can it be snowing?"

"It always snows early up here," he said, trying to reassure her.

"Yes, and always heavily. We're going to have a blizzard. We'll be stuck, snowbound."

"Nonsense, Wanda. They're only flurries—it'll be over in no time." She was blowing it out of proportion, as usual, he thought, and used his calmest tone to soothe her. But he couldn't help feel partly to blame.

Why had he planned this silly date? He'd had such hopes of pleasing her and ending their separation. Now his hopes were like those snowflakes, topsy-turvy and blowing in a chilly wind. He had to do something to turn this evening around.

She inched to his side. He felt her tremble against him, and wished it was he and not the wind that moved her so. Slowly, he draped his arm around her and pulled her closer. She didn't protest. In fact, she snuggled into him. He could feel her heart beating bold thumps that reverberated through his body. He squeezed her shoulder, turning the movement into a steady massage.

"Follow your own advice. Don't fight it…use it."

"Use it?" She pulled away, breaking the mood.

"The cozy cabin, the wine, the roaring fire."

"Sure…all we need are the marshmallows."

He took a stick from the wood box, wrapped a napkin around one end and stuck it in the fire. Immediately, it shot into flames. When he took it out, the ash it left fell off the end and floated upward on a warm air current.

"That's my trouble," he said. "Even as a scout, I always burned the marshmallows."

She laughed and rested her forehead on his chest. When she looked up again, the smokiness had returned to her eyes, and with it that smoldering undertow.

"Remind me to never take you camping," she said.

"Never take me camping. I hate camping. You have to sleep in separate bags." He kept his voice low and as steady as he could manage.

"Not always."

He turned and looked at her. The firelight spread a mellow glow over her face. He knew how her skin would feel; he longed to touch her. But he didn't dare. He already had his arm around her shoulder with her snuggled against his side. Any more contact would short-circuit his controls and he would sputter, hay-wire fast over the edge.

But then, she parted her lips, moving them, mouthing his name. He swayed.

This time she made the move, or did he? Their lips came together before he could tell. It didn't matter.

But it did; he had to stop her before it was too late.

"Wanda," he began. "There's something you should know...about tonight."

He could sense she wasn't listening. Her gaze was locked on his face, but her misty eyes saw nothing, he realized, nothing but promise.

Not that he didn't long to fulfill that promise. Every charged nerve begged to fulfill her need and his. But first, he had to make her understand.

"Wanda—"

"Later. Tell me later." Her fingers twisted through his hair. She pulled him closer. "Later," she said.

"Later," he repeated, hoping by then it would not be too late. He lowered his lips to hers and went hurling into bliss.

THIS WAS EXACTLY what she had been fighting. She could tell he wanted to kiss her. She knew she shouldn't let him, but for the life of her, she couldn't remember why. Then, before she could think, the opposite happened—she kissed him.

Their lips touched—first a brush, a teasing promise. She felt his warm breath caress her face, her neck. The fruity, winy smell of it proved more intoxicating than the drink itself.

She wavered on the edge of a cliff, passion beckoning her to jump. She closed her eyes as the feeling spiraled inside her, gaining force, making its way to the moist, sensitive essence of her sex.

What was he saying, "...something to tell you...?" She knew all she needed to know about tonight. She closed her eyes and, leaning forward, tumbling over the edge, she drew his lips to hers.

His mouth opened and covered hers. He pressed with an unrestrained force that roused her with its urgency. With his tongue, he parted her lips, and she opened, eagerly accepting him. A shudder weakened her as their tongues, dancing a ritual welcome, flicked and circled each other.

Her head spun. She floated, then sank, only to float again. She lost all sense of herself, not knowing where their connection began or ended. She gripped his arms, afraid she would melt, or slip away.

He embraced her, his body solid as he pressed against her. She was going nowhere. A warm familiar feeling spread over her, filling her with calm. She was a wayward soul who had found sanctuary, safe at last in the arms of home.

Then, she looked up and searched his face. He'd removed his glasses, and when she peered into his eyes, she saw them as if for the first time. They were so deep—a swimming pond created by crystal brown layers placed one upon another and another.

They formed a private pool that invited her to dive in and swim to its center...to home. Without glasses hiding his eyes, she imagined she could see past their glistening brown surface into his very heart and soul. Both of which were open as never before, ready to keep and hold her near.

In that moment, she knew their life together would change—that he finally understood what she so desperately had been trying to show him. She no longer feared he would desert her for his self-absorbed world of business and deadlines and goals. Their marriage was no longer in danger. They were safe.

With her fingertips, she traced the edges of his lips. "I love you." She mouthed the words in silence.

He kissed her fingers, her palm, and traveled down the inside of her arm, leaving a trail of moist kisses in his wake.

When he found his way to her chest, she arched upward, offering her breast as a pillow. He nestled there, warming her with his breath. The rich woodsy smell of the fire clung to his hair, and she buried her nose in his dark waves and immersed herself in its thick incense.

She ran her hands down his back, feeling the firmness of his muscles through his sweatshirt. Then she circled round his waist to his stomach and plunged down to the V between his thighs and the bulge straining against the seams of his new jeans.

When she took hold of him, he jumped as if trying to burst through the cloth barrier. His moans grew deep and raspy. He snapped his head back and let a sound escape from the bottom of his throat. Animal, so animal a sound. It strummed through her on a primal chord, leaving her resonating like a bell.

Suddenly, as though he could contain himself no longer, he plunged his face into the cushion of her chest, nibbling and sucking her breast through the flimsy, glittering gold that covered her.

She felt the zipper give way, a rush of chilly air as the dress slunk down around her waist. Then the warmth of the fire touched her bare skin. She shivered, but not from the cold. Her shiver started in her core from the quake of desire that rumbled through every cell in her body. She needed him. She wanted him. Now.

How could she have resisted so long?

She moved with urgency, unsnapping, unzipping. She pushed his jeans down to his knees, setting him free, then took him in her hands, caressing his silky flesh. He cried out, his lusty roar increasing her desire.

She slid beneath him, and with her dress hula-hooped around her waist, took hold and guided him inside her.

Home. In a borrowed cabin deep in the woods, she had finally returned home.

11

"I'VE NEVER WANTED you so much," he said, his own voice sounding raw. "So badly."

Her moan echoed through him, a soft needful sound he hadn't heard in months, but had dreamt of every night. She was here, in his arms. At last. Nothing else mattered—not Jackson, not his career, not his master plan. Being with her, and sharing, truly sharing, was all that mattered. And with his loving, he would tell her that. With his loving, he would take her home.

His hand trembled as he caressed her face. *I understand.* He whispered the words hoarsely in his mind. He'd tried to say them aloud, but his throat, and every other muscle in his body had contracted. Instead, he said it with his kisses, his caresses.

When she slipped underneath him, his whole body erupted in tingles. Her breath spread over his chest, warming him entirely. Slowly, she guided him to her opening and the heat from within drew him to her center.

He entered her with one driving thrust, and she arched upward welcoming him, her legs tight about his back, pulling him in farther. The feel of her around him—hot, demanding—ignited a wildness in him.

He wanted to go slowly, to savor each moment, but

the wildness took hold, a wildness he couldn't control. He kissed her with tongue and lips, savoring her womanly blend of salty sweat and arousal. The lemony smell of her perfume filled his head like a heavy rain cloud. He knew he would burst, yet he wanted to wait, to love her gently, slowly.

She echoed his passion, kissing and caressing him with such intensity, the fever inside him built. He answered it; his rhythmic thrust erupted into a driving frenzy, the crescendo building and building.

He gave one last thrust and felt her quake underneath him. He saw a bright flash and felt the tightness that had defined him for too long give way in a vast liberating release.

Together they collapsed in a melted tangle.

SHE OPENED HER EYES expecting to see Shangri-la. After all, that was how she felt, as if she rested in some wondrous paradise, wrapped in the arms of a sensual master of love. But her eyes wouldn't lie; she was indeed staring at John's chest. It was John, and not some exotic lover who had transported her to this utopia. He had made love to her as he'd never done before—passionately, freely. So out of control. And she'd loved every minute.

A rushing thrill skittered through her, suddenly making her aware of her body molded with his. With one leg still wrapped around his back and the other trapped under him, she couldn't move. Not that she wanted to. She lay quiet, savoring the touch of him. His hand cupped her buttocks; his chin rested just above her temple.

She listened to his breath coming in soft, steady currents as it spread warmth across her neck and shoulder. A mellowness fanned over her from the inside out. She was home, and being there never felt so good.

Suddenly he shifted, looked down with a soft apologetic smile, and rolled his weight off her. She gave a little cry as he eased away, then let her gaze travel over his body. A rumbling giggle built up inside. Though she tried to hold it back, the sight of him pulled the laugh right out.

She knew John dressed, or dressing or undressed. This John she'd never seen. His jeans and underpants hung down around one ankle, half hiding the socks he still wore. His sweatshirt had never made it over his head. It hung in a twisted loop around his neck. He looked about as un-Johnlike as possible, and at that moment, she could think of nothing more enticing.

She touched his shoulder, trying to delay his reaction until her giggling stopped and she could explain, but he pulled back. His eyes widened, then narrowed as a frown scarred his forehead. She watched the muscles in his neck tighten, and every inch of him retreat in defense.

"No...no. I'm not laughing. It's just..." She stopped and composed herself. "I love your new look."

He gave himself a quick once-over and shrugged, but the frown didn't leave his face.

Oh, no. Now I've done it.

Slowly a slanted smile crossed his lips, and she immediately recognized Rocko.

"Laugh all you want, sweetheart, but you aren't exactly dressed for a society ball, either."

Wanda glanced down at herself and gasped. Dusty's beautiful liquid, gold dress pooled about her middle like a wide belt. She was naked from the waist up and the waist down. In fact, her foot, with yellow lacy panties dangling from the toe, was her only other covered body part. Talk about spontaneous, she thought, and laughed at the wanton image she cut.

"So tell me," Wanda said. "Should we dress or undress for dinner?"

"Why bother?" With that he pulled the afghan from the love seat, threw it around them and passed her the cheese.

THERE WASN'T MUCH to clean up after they finished. The plates were unused, and aside from some crumbs and a smear of wine in each glass, nothing remained of their picnic. They sprawled back against the love seat and flipped a coin to see who would use the shower first. Wanda won and entered the small bathroom, determined hers would be the fastest shower on record.

When she stepped out of the bathroom, the living room had been transformed—all evidence of their meal gone, as well as the love seat. In its place was a bed—small, cozy and inviting with the army blanket spread over it. Her dress and his clothes hung neatly over the backs of two kitchen chairs.

"There are advantages to being married to an old Boy Scout," she said. For once his orderliness elated her. He had turned a borrowed cabin into a cozy refuge. He smiled, kissed her on the forehead and slipped into the bathroom.

Wanda warmed herself before the fire, knowing she didn't need to. The initial chill she felt upon leaving the steamy bathroom had long been burned away by the glowing flame inside her—the flame John had ignited. Tonight he'd allowed himself to burst free of his usual constraints and proprieties. Tonight, he'd lost himself and her right along with him.

She gazed into the fire, at the flames caressing the logs. They were like yellow-and-red fingers, delicate yet powerful. Magic, she thought. Some of that magic must have entered the two of them. *Yep, magic and spice. I couldn't have planned it better myself.*

But this hadn't been planned, and that's what made it so perfect.

And John had finally understood. His response to the situation they'd found themselves in had been undeniably spontaneous. And as for her response to him, there was only one way to describe it. She had spontaneously combusted.

The thought seemed to heat her skin to the point of stinging. No, it was the fire. How long had she been standing there? She'd gone beyond warming to actually burning herself.

Hurrying from the hearth, she jumped into the bed, slid between the covers and waited, her attention fixed on the bathroom door.

John stepped out and hastened to the fireplace, first warming his front. The yellow glow bathed his naked body; wetness glistened on his damp skin. She studied the body she knew so well and reveled in the pleasure its familiarity gave her.

His wet hair dripped beads of water down his back. When he turned around, she traced one droplet over his muscular chest, past his taut belly and down until it was lost in a shadow of hairs. Their gazes met and locked.

"Yee...ouch!" John grabbed his buttocks and

jumped forward. "Marshmallows aren't all I tend to burn," he said, looking at the fire and rubbing his backside.

"I can't guarantee it'll be any cooler in here." She raised the covers, inviting him in.

He practically dived into the bed and proceeded to cover her with nibbly kisses and tickles. Her giggles filled the room. She twisted and turned, knotting the sheets about her. Her legs kicked madly, but her arms were immobile, trapped by the bedclothes and his solid body.

"Stop, John. Stop." She could barely get the words out. Her breathing was no more than little gasps. "You're wild."

Finally he stopped, and she lay exhausted with him leaning over her. His eyes sparkled, his face was flushed, and his damp hair was slicked to his head. A rivulet trailed its way from his hairline down to his jaw and pooled at his chin. In slow motion it fell and splotched on her chest.

The sudden coldness was unexpected. She gave a short cry and jerked.

"What's the matter? Scared of a little water?" With that he lowered his head, shaking and flinging water everywhere.

Wanda laughed with her eyes scrunched shut. "My goodness. You are wild!"

"Yet another reason not to take me camping. It brings out the animal in me."

"I'll say. Who are you? What have you done with my husband?"

"That old stick? Don't worry, sweetheart. The boss had us take care of him so he won't be bothering you anymore."

"Oh," she said, perhaps a bit too nostalgically.

John frowned and a cloud of worry crossed his eyes. "Disappointed?" he asked in his own voice.

She shook her head and eased her hands from under the sheets. Taking his face in her hands, she slowly pulled him closer. She could taste his lips before they touched hers, taste the faint brinish tang they had even after a shower. She could feel them—wet, warm and eager—before they molded over her mouth.

She inhaled, breathing in the fresh-bathed smell of him, and opened her mouth to meet his—first in a mere grazing, the tips of their tongues playing tag.

When he deepened their kiss, pressing his mouth over hers in a slow, savoring manner, her senses surged like a river flooding over its dam. Her head swam and her body was carried away in a rushing current of desire and love. They held on to each other as he untangled the covers and stretched himself naked alongside her.

The contact, his warm body touching her skin, sent tingle after tingle breaking all over her. She parted her legs, making a space for him to nestle, and when he did, she arched up to meet him, eager to recapture the fever of their earlier lovemaking. But he shook his head and with his pelvis, slowly pressed her down onto the mattress.

"We've got all the time in the world," he whispered in a mellow bass that strummed every chord in her.

Her moan sounded like a purr, curling around in her throat.

"I'm going to make this last until daybreak," he said.

She closed her eyes and wished for a long night.

12

WHEN WANDA AWOKE the next morning, she wasn't sure where she was. She lay on her stomach in bed. Whose bed? Her limbs sprawled in every direction, but they didn't seem to be attached to her. They felt limp, floating. Never before had she felt so peaceful, so relaxed.

Then she remembered their night of lovemaking, her night of rediscovery. *John.* She smiled and turned over to embrace him.

The space was empty and cold. Wanda shot upright.

"John," she called, her voice echoing in the chilly air.

She looked around the room. The fire had burned out, which explained the cold. She quickly glanced at the kitchen chair. Only her dress hung there. His clothes were missing, which partly explained the empty space in bed.

"John," she tried again. No chance he was in the shower and couldn't hear her.

Pulling the blanket around herself, Wanda climbed out of bed and began searching. She knocked on the bathroom door and opened it. Empty, just as she suspected. Other than that room, there were no other places he could be and not hear her calling.

"So where is he?" she asked, looking about the space.

Sunlight poured through the glass wall and filled the cabin with a cheery brightness. Wanda felt anything but cheery. How could he leave her all alone, sleeping in a strange bed in some stranger's house? What if the owner appeared and found her there? How could she explain breaking and entering?

She stared out the picture windows, squinting against the glare. The blizzard she had feared had been only that, a fear. Only a faint dusting of snow covered the ground. The little blue boat, sprinkled white, sat quietly with its motor lifted out of the water. The lake winked a thousand glittering hellos to her.

A smaller cabin she hadn't noticed by moonlight peeked from between the pines on the opposite shore. An elderly man, fishing pole in one hand, catch in the other, walked toward the roundish woman waiting at the end of his pier. Arms linked, they walked the winding path up to their cabin.

Such a charming picture. She thought about John and herself at retirement age and closed her eyes dreamily. Would they be as loving, she wondered? After last night, she felt certain they would.

She gazed back across the lake in time to see the couple turn and look in her direction. Her muscles tensed. Had they seen her? No. The sun was bouncing off the glass; no way could they see into the cabin. But then, the man pointed, his aim and focus zeroing right in on her.

Wanda jumped, gathered her blanket and rushed from the window. Just what she needed, to be spotted by the neighbors. Last night she would have welcomed being rescued, but in the light of day, discovery presented a different set of circumstances. Different and awkward.

If this couple were anything like her elderly relatives—overly protective and safety conscious—they would call the police. Explaining her presence to the owner would be difficult enough. Explaining unlawful entry to a small-town sheriff could prove hazardous to her freedom. A night in a stranger's cabin was one thing, but a night in jail...

She stared blankly as a film clouded her vision, obscuring the room and its details. She tried to swallow but found her throat blocked.

Control. Get control, girl. Think of how John would react. Logically. Think this through logically. Chances were they hadn't seen her, and even if they had, they couldn't have seen clearly from such a distance. She could be anyone...a houseguest or even the owner.

Besides, even if they got suspicious, how likely were they to come investigating? Not very, she concluded, and took a deep breath. She could feel her heartbeat slowing to its normal rhythm. The invisible fingers that had been pinching her throat released, allowing her to swallow.

She looked around, seeing the room and its light-colored furnishings again. With this regained calm, her original thoughts returned. John. Where could he be?

If she had to explain her squatter status, she preferred doing so with him by her side. Better still, she would let John do the honors. If the last few minutes were any indication, she would surely get excited and overexplain them right into a jail cell. In any case, no one's explanation would go over well with her dressed in a blanket.

She walked into the kitchen, grabbed her clothes off the chair, and noticed a note laying flat on the table. She picked it up and read: "Gone for gas. The main road isn't too far away so I shouldn't be gone long. Didn't have the heart to wake you, and if I had...well, let's just say I wouldn't be out in search of civilization if I had. Love you."

Gone for gas. Wanda smiled to herself. John the hero. Forever the scout. She had to admit, it was charming. She also had to admit he was right about not waking her.

Instantly she felt a stirring, and found herself wishing he had roused her from sleep, with kisses. A warm glow blossomed inside her. Wanda wrapped the blanket tighter, trying to prolong the feeling, but the chill of the room fought her.

John wasn't around to warm her with his embraces, and since she didn't want to freeze, she had to think practically. The room needed heating. A nice fire meant smoke billowing like a signal from the chimney. The neighbors couldn't miss that, but possibly the smoke would convince them she belonged. What trespasser would draw such attention to herself? So a fire it would be. There was only one problem: she would have to rebuild the darn thing herself.

Not a problem. Hadn't she watched John do it last night? But he had taken so long just setting up. She was freezing; she couldn't waste time being that meticulous. Besides, what did it matter if the logs were stacked neatly or not?

She dropped her dress on the table and crossed to the fireplace, her covers trailing behind her like a wedding toga. She knelt before the hearth and threw the wood in. A box of extra long matches rested against the stones. She lit one and tossed it atop her pile. Nothing. She lit another and watched it glow and die.

After her fifth attempt, she was ready to throw in the remaining matches and light them all. Surely that would work. Instead she decided to give John's method a try, and did a mental run-through of his technique. Little chips at the bottom, small branches next, and largest logs last.

The blaze started on the first attempt. There was merit to John's systematic approach after all. Maybe she could start becoming more systematic herself...in moderation, of course. *And let's start now,* she thought, ticking off a to-do list. A shower, a quick tidy up of the room and then she would see what was left of last night's feast.

Wanda picked up her gold evening outfit and shook her head. Walking around in the bright cabin in that dress, she would feel like a glow worm caught in the noonday sun. Too bad she hadn't dressed more casually, but how was she to know she'd be out all night? She'd certainly had no intention of spending the night in a stranger's hideaway. She definitely hadn't planned on spending the night with John, but here she was, a victim of her own spontaneity.

Well, *victim* wasn't the right word, she thought, remembering the night and John's unbridled passion. *Lottery winner* better described how she felt. She giggled. Yes, lottery winner for sure. After all those months of reruns of the same discussion, after all her glitch-ridden schemes and all her agony, everything was solved so quickly and unexpectedly. Hip-hip-hooray for life's pleasant little surprises.

Now that things were settled, they would drive straight to Dusty's so she could pick up her things and then they would head home. Nothing would put their lives on hold ever again. Nothing they wouldn't be able to work out.

A loud grumble in her stomach interrupted her daydream. Eating suddenly took priority over showering. She searched the kitchen, but found nothing. She looked around, saw their picnic basket tucked behind the loft stairs, and crossed the room, hoping it wasn't as empty as the cabinets.

It wasn't. John had repacked the remains of their dinner. Unfortunately, it contained nothing edible. She rummaged through, rearranging the neat layers, pushing aside the empty wine bottles, crumpled wrappers, the folded paper bag that once held bread. The glasses clinked against each other and the plates as she dug to the bottom of the wicker tote. She rocked back on her heels and groaned.

She hoped John would have better luck finding a gas station than she'd had finding food. But if he didn't, they needn't starve. They could always go fishing. Someone was doing just that, she thought as she listened to a droning motor out on the lake.

The noise grew louder, more distinct. Wanda stood, clutching the basket shieldlike in front of her. The boat drew closer to her pier. There was no mistaking its occupants.

The elderly fisherman and his wife maneuvered to the dock and tied their craft opposite the blue boat. Horrified, Wanda watched as the man clambered out and helped his much larger wife do the same. Suddenly, they no longer looked so charming. They looked downright threatening.

She stayed frozen for only a second before turning left...right...left, pivoting, ricocheting off her own indecision like a target in a carnival shooting gallery.

Hide. Hide. But where? The place was much too open—a regular fishbowl and she was the fish about to be hooked. The couple was bounding toward the house, not slow-stepping as their age would dictate. Just her luck to have Jack and Jill LaLanne paying a call.

Behind the love seat seemed the most likely hiding place. Wanda spun around and bolted only two steps before her twisted toga snared her like a well-cast line. The picnic basket crashed to the floor, its contents spilling across the polished planks.

Frantically, she scooped up plates, glasses and napkins, tossing them back into their hamper. Breaking glass shattered the quiet. Noise. She was making too much noise, but she couldn't be any more silent.

Sweat dampened her forehead. She heard her own voice, high-pitched and breathy, repeating the same words over and over. "Oh, no. Oh, no." She circled the space on her knees, retrieving picnic items and ignoring the dull pain that rewarded each step.

Rap, rap, rap. The unmistakable sound of knuckles tapping glass. Wanda froze. Behind the glass wall, with the morning sun providing dramatic stage lighting, stood the neighbors—Mr. and Mrs. Doomsday. It was too late to hide, and too late to come up with a believable alibi. Stuck with the truth, she could only hope they would buy it.

"My, my, my," said the man when Wanda opened the sliding door. He turned to his wife. "Isn't she lovely?" he asked, punctuating his words with jerky movements that reminded Wanda of a chicken pecking the air. He jerked back to face her.

Lovely? Wanda blinked then stared down into his twinkling eyes and a drawn little face that matched his slight body. A possible perpetrator wrapped in a blanket...lovely?

"I had to come over and meet you," he continued.

"Couldn't help himself." The wife twisted her mouth and glanced down at her husband, her eyebrows arching on cue. "I couldn't stop him, so I came along to make sure he leaves. Like right now...the poor girl isn't even dressed."

"She's fine. She has on a blanket," he said. "Can't ask anymore of a honeymooner. Remember ours?" His eyebrows did a Groucho dance.

"We went camping in February. I lived in long johns and a snowsuit," the woman said, folding her three chins into her neck.

"Honeymooner?" Wanda looked from man to wife.

"Oh, we know your little secret. Larry had already closed the cabin for the season, so when we saw him out here last week, we boated over to check—"

"To nose about," the wife corrected.

"—and that's when Larry told us he'd loaned the cabin out to a honeymooning couple," he said, not missing a beat.

"Larry?" Wanda asked. "Larry who?"

"Why, Larry Shu. The new owner of this house."

"He *also* said not to disturb them," the woman added.

"Who's disturbing? I'm being neighborly. And I

brought a gift." With that, he raised two trout up to Wanda's face.

Immediately, the smell of briny weeds and ammonia choked her. It didn't matter that they were freshly caught fish from a freshwater lake. She knew anything dead, slimy and staring at her in glassy-eyed wide-mouthed surprise should smell. Her head swam. She rocked backwards slightly.

"Take those things out of her face," the woman scolded. "You're making her sick."

"No. No, I'm fine. Come…come in. Uh…make yourselves comfortable while I change. So much to talk about…like Larry. Imagine, you know Larry," Wanda said, her voice no more than a choked whisper. She accepted the trout and slid the door closed behind her guests.

She held the two hooked fish up and glared at them, eyeball to eyeball. *Imagine that.*

A distinct fishy odor permeated the room, but it had nothing to do with the catch of the day.

As SHE WATCHED her guests motor back across the lake, she was surprised how cold and drained she felt. How could he, she wondered? The entire time, he had no intention of taking her issues seriously. It was just as she had thought, exactly what she had always accused him of—humoring her, making her think he was making a serious effort to change. Promise her anything, then get her back home to his same old unacceptable behavior.

And the one way to accomplish that, the one way to distract her from her goal was to get her in bed. It hadn't taken much effort on his part, either.

He had lied! The whole spontaneous evening had

been totally planned: the roundabout drive to nowhere, running out of gas, the car trunk without his
usual emergency provisions. All planned.

The rumble started in her head and in no time she
was shaking uncontrollably. Lies! All lies!

She started questioning everything about their
"date," and it dawned on her that there probably
hadn't even been a play. Who ever heard of an outdoor theater open this late in the season? She should
have checked, but why would she? If it had been anyone else suggesting an evening al fresco, she would
have suspected they were confused, or they had the
wrong theater or the wrong date.

But not John. He never made such mistakes. She
always relied on him to sort out those types of details.

A cold chill gripped her. Her stomach knotted with
fistlike tightness. Last night's new and wonderful unbridled passion had been calculated also. He had even
lied about that!

Her shaking stopped just as every bit of blood
drained from her head. She felt weak, dizzy. She
grabbed hold of the fireplace, and watched with de-
tached interest as the floor zoomed toward her face,
receded and zoomed in again.

I will not faint, she told herself. She couldn't. John
would return soon, and she had to face him with a
clear, level head.

Unsteadily, she made her way to the bathroom and
turned on both faucets full force. She splashed hand-
fuls of water on her face—first the hot, then the cold.
She ended by plunging her face into the filled basin.

She walked back into the living room, rubbing her
face with a rough towel, less to dry herself than to
toughen her resolve. She would not get hysterical. She

would not throw any objects. She would present the evidence calmly, coolly. She would listen to his logical explanations, and when he finished, she would pronounce him guilty.

A click echoed across the room. The doorknob turned, the door swung open and John bounced into the room, carrying two small white grocery bags. He was flushed from exercise, his eyes bright and sparkling. His smile took over his face. He looked like someone who had signed the deal of a lifetime.

"Hi, sweetheart," he said, crossing to the kitchen.

He placed the bags on the table, pulled his wallet and keys from his pants pockets and placed them beside the packages. Greasy spots dotted one bag, turning the white to shiny translucent blotches. From the other came the distinct aroma of coffee, an odor which invaded the room like dark toxic fumes.

13

"YOU'LL NEVER GUESS what I found," he said.

"A gas station." Her voice sounded flat.

"Yes, but something even better. You'll never—"

"Coffee and crescents." This time she couldn't keep the bite out of her tone.

"Right." His raised eyebrows were the only indication he noticed anything, but he continued as though he hadn't. "From a great little deli and it was only—"

"Thirty minutes away," she said, slicing his sentence in two. "A little town called Perry. Knowing Larry's talent for arranging things, I'm sure he also drew you an excellent map."

She watched the smile slide away, pulling his muscles and setting his face in a gaunt expression.

"Wanda, I can explain."

"Explain!" she screamed, throwing the towel at him. "Liars don't explain—they lie."

The damp cloth sailed across the space like a screwball. Too wide to hit him, it dropped low and flopped into the coffee. The bag tumbled over. Cream-lightened liquid flowed everywhere and dripped onto the floor.

"Explain *that* to Larry. And while you're at it, you can explain why your plan backfired."

She looked around for something else to throw.

There was nothing, so she took off her shoe and hurled that. John ducked and the shoe thumped against the far wall.

She was trying to remove the other pump when John grabbed her by the shoulders, almost knocking her off balance.

"I tried to tell you…last night, but you didn't want to talk. You said talk would spoil the moment."

"And you agreed quickly enough."

"I hoped it could wait until tomorrow."

"Tomorrow over coffee and rolls, tomorrow after we got back to D.C., or tomorrow as in never?" She shook herself free and pushed him away, surprised by her strength. "You've lied about everything. Why should I believe you now?"

"I didn't lie about last night. There was nothing false about what either of us were experiencing."

To prove his point he moved in on her. She could feel the heat of his body seep into her pores. Suddenly the memory of their lovemaking washed over her, flooding her reason and leaving her melting in wet desire.

She closed her eyes, shaking her head, trying to chase the memory and the feeling away, but he took her chin in one hand and held her still. With his thumb, he rubbed her lips until she felt them relax.

She tried to resist, tried to remain strong, but a faint whimper was her only voice of protest. He covered her mouth with his, and silenced even that.

She felt his lips press gently, moving hers apart. She kissed him back, then opened her mouth to accept his probing tongue. Her legs felt wobbly. Her stomach flipped over as wave after wave of excitement hit.

Again images of the past night flooded her senses.

This was how she felt when John made love to her. Last night. The thought echoed. Wanda stiffened.

Last night was a lie and she had so easily been taken in then...and now. No, not now.

She twisted out of his embrace, angry with herself for being so easily manipulated, angry at her body for betraying her. And angry at John for knowing which of her buttons to push and for pushing them.

"How do I know what you were feeling last night? You had everything else calculated down to the smallest detail, why not your lovemaking?"

"You could tell it was special. It was different."

"Very different. Just different enough to make me think you had changed, that you wanted to change. But it was all a performance, wasn't it? You're the same control freak you were when I left home."

"What was I supposed to do? You weren't satisfied with any effort I made. I'm beginning to doubt you ever will be."

"So now it's my fault. You lie and deceive me and it's all my fault," she said, pacing behind the table.

"You were the one complaining. You were the one so unhappy." He jabbed his finger at her as he spoke. "Well, I have news for you. Everything was fine until you decided it needed changing."

"It did need changing. We were stuck."

"And now what are we?"

"Hopeless," she said. The word shocked her.

Quiet settled over the room. John shifted, his focus never leaving her face, but his eyes seemed to darken as if closing behind a heavy invisible door.

"Why did you do...this?" She looked around her as she asked, her arms outstretched, palms up. "Why fake all this?"

"I had to get you alone...let you see what you meant to me. I tried making adjustments, even though you didn't seem interested in making any of your own. You kept on about being spontaneous."

The rasp in his voice made her pause. Could it be remorse? She hoped so.

"So you plan a fake stranding in the woods?" she asked.

"I gave you spontaneous." His voice bit through the air.

"You gave me a lie," she said, angry all over again, this time for foolishly thinking she'd heard an apology. "How could you?"

"You're not listening."

"I don't want to listen anymore. And I don't want to be stranded here with you, for real or otherwise." Wanda rushed to the kitchen table, grabbed John's keys and hurried to the sliding door.

"I'll show you stranded and spontaneous all wrapped up in one crazy act." She slid the door open and pitched the keys as far as she could. The yard in back of the house grew wild with brambles. The keys nestled in the top of a bush then sank deep into the twisted branches.

Wanda shot out the doorway and didn't look back until she was at the far end of the pier. She saw John bending and searching, bending and searching. He pushed the thicket aside, jerked his hand out and threw his finger into his mouth.

Now that's what I call stranded, she thought, as she untied the boat and climbed in. She tried starting the motor, but it kicked over once and stopped. She glanced back to the house. John had abandoned the key search and was racing toward her. She pulled the cord again, and again it sputtered and died.

''Wanda!'' He had reached the pier.

She took a deep breath and pulled. This time, the motor kicked in. She moved the gear lever and puttered away just as he reached out to grab her. The motor roared, but it didn't drown out the sound of John splashing into the lake.

Wanda turned her back to him and steered the boat away.

She wasn't sure where she was going until she caught sight of the elderly couple standing on the opposite shore, staring in her direction. She pointed the boat a little to the right and headed toward them.

14

"I'D BE THE FIRST ONE to admit I've made a mess," Wanda said, sinking so low into the full bathtub, the water touched her chin. She blew the bubbles away from her nose and cast a side glance at her sister.

Dusty, sitting next to the tub on the little stool usually reserved for towels, twisted a lock of hair around her finger and remained silent.

"Go ahead and say it."

"Say what?" Dusty asked.

"That my schemes never work."

"Can't. It was John's scheme this time. Imagine, using that out-of-gas routine. Who would fall for that?"

"I didn't fall for it...not really. I called him a liar."

"Good for you. Anyone going along with that old ploy wants to be tricked."

"What do you mean by that?" Wanda said, sitting up.

"And then trapping you in some old dilapidated shack."

"It wasn't dilapidated; it was brand-new, and very cozy. And I wasn't trapped. It wasn't as though he had keys and locked me in."

"But he got you there under false pretenses. Who ever heard of an outdoor theater being open this late in the season? No, he was a real cad, and deserved everything you threw at him."

"My shoe. I threw my shoe, and I threw his car keys in the bushes." Wanda, suddenly feeling very heavy, slid back into the water.

"Good," said Dusty.

"And I called him all kinds of names, and said things I can't even remember. I was so mad."

"He earned them, and he earned your anger. The nerve, taking you to an isolated spot and seducing you. What would make him use such despicable tactics?"

"He was desperate. It was our last date and he was trying to show me he could change, that he cared."

"Planned spontaneity. Only John could come up with that one."

"Well, he tried," Wanda said sitting upright again and glaring at her sister.

"Uh-huh."

"Besides, he didn't seduce me. I seduced him." Wanda noticed Dusty's eyebrow arch, and rushed on. "He was trying to tell me, but I kept stopping him. I didn't want to talk...I wanted... Oh, Dusty, it was so perfect. How could I have doubted him? Why did I say all those things to him?"

"I would guess because you're rash, impulsive and you're—"

"Point made. I blew it."

"Good!"

"What?" She couldn't believe her ears. Her sister was happy about the disastrous state of her affairs.

"I said *good,*" she repeated and reaching over, placed a hand atop Wanda's head and pushed her under.

Wanda surfaced, spitting and sputtering. She stared at Dusty. "What was that for?"

"For finally seeing the light. You love John and he loves you. Maybe you both need to make a few changes, but who doesn't? Now that you've got each other's attention, start working. But no more schemes and no more drastic measures."

"You're right. No more of my schemes. I'll sit down and talk, I'll be calm and logical and rational, and—"

"Hey. Don't get carried away. No one's expecting miracles, just moderation."

Wanda climbed from the tub and secured an over-size towel around her.

"Right, just moderation. What shall I do? Call? Yes, I'll call him right away."

She grabbed Dusty up off the stool, swooped her into a bear hug, then apologized when she noticed how wet she'd gotten her. Wanda knotted her towel tighter, headed for the door and froze.

"He's probably mad at me. Do you think he'll want to talk? What if he's still at the cabin looking for the keys?"

"He's an old Boy Scout—he's found the keys. And yes, he'll talk. He may be mad, but he'll talk."

"Oh, Dusty," she said, moving to hug her sister again.

Dusty threw her hands up, blocking the embrace. "Enough of this secondhand water—I'll wait for my Saturday bath, thank you. Go on, make the call."

Just then the doorbell chimed and repeated itself before the first sounds had ended. The two sisters looked at each other.

"John," Wanda whispered, and rushed for the door.

So many thoughts flashed in her head as she ran through the living room. Would he forgive her? What should she say first? Or should she say nothing and just kiss him? What was he doing—resting on the bell? The noise hadn't stopped for one second. Was he that eager to see her, too?

She flung the door open and jumped back with a gasp.

There he stood, almost as tall as the door frame. His clothes were damp, muddy, and hanging askew on his body. His eyeglasses perched on the end of his nose, the frame broken and one lens shattered. His hair was tossed wildly on his head and his face was pinched. The muscle in his left jaw twitched. He looked like a madman with his arm raised and fist poised to pound. What? The door? Her head?

"About time," he said and pushed past her.

"John, what happened?"

A growl escaped before he answered. "Tornado Wanda happened. And I was too naive to run for cover."

"I'm so sorry..."

"Well so am I, sweetheart. Sorry I ever agreed to this whole thing. I must need my head examined. I'm crazy. Yeah, you've driven me crazy. What made me think I could ever change enough to please you?"

"But you have changed. I *am* pleased," she said, watching him pace and fearing he didn't hear her.

"You want to know what happened to me? As if you didn't know. That nice little old couple from across the lake. Remember them? Mr. and Mrs. Concerned Citizen? They called the cops."

"What?"

"Yeah, you heard right, the cops. And don't act surprised. It was whatever you told them that set them off."

"I didn't tell them anything," she said weakly. "Nothing that would interest the police."

"Obviously they had a different impression and so did the cops!" John's voice boomed.

The soothing bass fiddle she knew had changed into a boiling-over kettle drum, and its vibration shook every fiber of her.

"Yep, the law came and when they showed up, I was burrowed in the sticker bushes. Imagine what an innocent picture that made. Imagine trying to convince two cops about as bright as your average sitcom character that your wife threw your car keys in the brier patch...on purpose." He started pacing.

"Oh, no."

"No is right, because that's not all."

Of course that wouldn't be all. Things were bad, and simply because she wished the opposite, she knew they would get worse. Why hadn't she listened to Dusty?

John paced the room but stopped short right in front of her.

"I spent the past five hours in jail," he said, "for trespassing, breaking and entering and deserting my vehicle in the middle of an access road. They probably would have held me longer if they could."

She was almost afraid to ask, "How did you get out?"

"Larry. My one phone call. It took him three hours to get there, but I used the time wisely. I thought about you and what I was going to do when—" He stopped and growled.

The sound pierced her, and she backed away, shivering from a cold she'd never known before.

"You can't really mean that, not after last night?"

He stopped, walked away, then turned and faced her.

"Yes, I can," he said. "For all I know, last night was another part of your grand scheme."

"Scheme?" She couldn't believe what she was hearing. John's circuits had overloaded. He was sputtering garbage.

"I was the one saying whoa. You were the one making the moves. The only real thing I'm sure about is that I've had enough. Living with you is like riding a whirlwind. Well, I prefer something a bit more tame," he said, pacing again. "And housebroken...and conservative. Boring, even. But whatever it is, it isn't you."

He started walking toward the door.

She had to stop him, but her voiced was jailed in her throat and her legs felt shackled to the floor. She had to stop him from walking out that door, but she was prisoner of her own panic.

She tried again to speak. Instead she whimpered, but it was enough.

John stopped and turned. He tilted his head; his face screwed up with lines of confusion. This was her chance, she must speak now or never. She must.

"You're so off the scale," he said while she still struggled to free her voice. "You wouldn't be happy until you have me walking upside down on the ceiling. Well, as foolish as it sounds, I tried doing just that and fell on my damn head. I want to be normal again. I want my boring, normal, boxed-up life back. No more surprises, no more spice, and if that's what it takes, no more Wanda!''

''John, please listen. I know I've said things I didn't really mean. Please, don't you do the same. Don't say something we'll both be sorry for.''

''I'm already sorry. Sorry I ever met you. Sorry I thought it would ever work out. And I'm damned sorry I ever said, 'I do.' Can't get any sorrier.'' With that he stormed for the door.

''No, wait. We have to talk—''

''The only talking we'll do is through my lawyer.''

''No!'' Inertia fled. She rushed across the room.

''Yes! And one last thing.''

He paused, his index finger rigid and pointed at her as he looked her up and down. She thought she saw a softening in his eyes, a relaxing of the muscles in his face and neck. He began lowering his hand. Slowly. His finger flexed.

She released her breath and stepped into his space. She reached up, touching him, stroking his arm.

''Ohhh,'' he said, sounding more like a trapped animal than her John.

She felt him stiffen, then he backed away. Again the finger pointed at her face. He held his position in silence.

Wanda held her breath.

''Put some clothes on,'' he snapped, and walked out, slamming the door behind him.

15

WANDA CHECKED THE CLOCK on the dashboard. Five o'clock and it was already dusk. Sure, she could have blamed the rain and the clouds for the afternoon blackness, but she knew better. She couldn't even blame the encroaching winter. No, her mood and her mood alone caused this darkness to settle around her.

Rain pattered on the roof of her convertible. The wipers, working overtime, did nothing to improve visibility, so she squinted through the waterfall and eased the car into her driveway.

The headlights flashed on the living room windows, sending a harsh glare back into her eyes. She blinked, killed the engine, then ran through the downpour, house keys at the ready.

She stepped inside to more darkness, expertly skirted the furniture and walked to the kitchen.

"I'm home," she said to the refrigerator after flicking on the ceiling light. In a husky Lauren Bacall voice, she added, "Not talking today, huh? Mad I'm late? Couldn't help it…the meeting ran over. I know, I know. I said that the last time. What do you prefer, a lie?"

Who would? She hadn't and look what it had earned her, a return ticket to an empty house.

She could have stayed in Richmond. Dusty had

begged her to, claiming she would miss Wanda if she left. At least someone would, but she moved anyway.

No need ignoring the facts—she and John were finished. She no longer had him in her life. Instead, she had the house, and he had a sublet in the city. She was alone and the best way to get used to that was to live alone.

"Right, fridge?" she said, grabbing a carton of ice cream, a spoon and moving to her office. She sat at the desk and began licking down chocolate fudge, hoping the caffeine would ease her headache. No such luck.

Massaging her temples didn't work, either. Another migraine. She had them frequently now, ever since she started putting in more hours at work.

Even though her home office idea had proved successful, she did more car commuting than telecommuting. Now that she had her flex time, she didn't need it, didn't want it. She wanted John.

Wanda squinted at her desk calendar. One month and four days exactly, she thought, picking up a pencil and crossing off the day. She never knew time could drag by so slowly and still seem like only yesterday.

Best laid plans gone astray. Isn't that what Granny would say? That and be careful what you wish for. She had only wished to get back the husband she used to know. She still wished for that.

"Whoa, sweetheart," she whispered, low and throaty.

A Hollywood moll answered in a tough voice that grated like sandpaper.

I can see that you're about to take a dangerous turn. I can hear your gray cells revving up.

"You're wrong. This lady has learned her lesson."

So explain the ice cream. Double chocolate fudge, right? A little scheming inducement? Admit it—you miss him.

"Sure, I miss him," she said aloud, staring blankly and tracing her lips with the eraser tip. She sighed. "If I could get past his lawyers, I'd tell him."

Hey, what's a few lawyers up against a pro like yourself? You could work out a scheme—

"No schemes. I promised everyone, including myself...no more schemes."

But you love him. Look how you're suffering. I bet he is, too. You know he still loves you. All he needs is to see you in the flesh. Where's the scheme in that?

She shivered. "Flesh, huh?" she said, puffing on the pencil and blowing imaginary smoke rings. "That would be harder to arrange than a photo-op with The Phantom."

Yeah, but what've you got to lose?

What indeed? She'd already lost John and he was all that mattered. She could at least *try* to meet with him. It would take planning—some of the best creative planning she'd ever done.

If she failed, he would be irate, but he was already angrily pursuing a divorce. He couldn't get any angrier and he certainly couldn't divorce her twice. If she didn't even try, he would certainly divorce her once, and once was all it took.

Instantly, her headache vanished. She pulled out the large city directory and reached for the phone. John's birthday was two days away. She'd already mailed a card, but he needed something a bit more personal. Smiling, she punched the numbers. She would send him a greeting with *Wanda* written all over it.

JOHN SAT AT HIS DESK, staring at his appointment book and drawing circles around the day's date. One month, four days and... He glanced at his new wristwatch. And too many hours. If he had found it difficult living through these past weeks, what made him think he could survive a divorce? Divorce was final. Divorce meant a lifetime of no Wanda, no more crooked smiles, no more teasing stares and no more challenges.

John rested his chin on his fist and looked out the window. He was crazy to think he could live without her. Exist maybe, but not live. Every night since their split, he had worked later and later, hating returning to his sublet. The cramped studio felt emptier than their house had been after Wanda's furniture trick.

His world was gray now; totally devoid of excitement. He longed for the chaos of one of her schemes. In fact, he'd fully expected her to try halting the divorce proceedings with one of her crazy plots. When she didn't, he felt cut in half by a paring knife.

"Get over it, Rocko—you'll live." The snide voice escaped from the side of his mouth.

"Exist," he corrected. "If you haven't noticed, there isn't much living in my life these days."

"Live, exist. Don't get literary. You got your business...that's what you wanted. Hey, you're even going to be top Erectoman. No dame telling you to slow down. No criticizing. You want any of that back?"

No.

The answer struck in his brain like a bell. That's what had started all this in the first place, Wanda's plans, Wanda's scheme to shake some excitement into him, as if he were a pot of bland stew.

Maybe he needed some changing, but her demands were extreme. She would never be satisfied. To her, he would always be an interesting painting that could use more yellow here, more red there.

Painful as it was, this divorce was for the best. He would just have to live with that.

John took a deep breath and noisily exhaled. He had to concentrate. In less than two hours, Jackson would be pushing through the office door, eager to see the final drawings.

He looked at the building plans stretched out in front of him. Twenty-four floors of bold, clean lines guaranteed not to shock the viewer. What he saw, he would define as stability, security. No one but Wanda would see a box.

"IT LOOKS LIKE A BOX," Jackson said. "After all this time, I was expecting something...different."

"This room is papered with all the *something different*." Larry's voice quavered on its climb into the falsetto range.

"Yes, and they're all variations on the same theme." Jackson pointed to the sketches on the wall. "The glass box, the granite-and-exposed-steel box. And this one with the indoor jungle...the tree box."

"You said simplicity, you got simplicity," Larry said.

"I didn't say boring." He turned from Larry and focused on John. "Rockman, I thought you people could deliver. Your earlier work impressed me and I wanted to give you a chance."

"You wanted a bargain," Larry said under his breath.

Normally, John would have cut his partner a silencing look, but this time he didn't bother. He was glad to see Jackson go. Now he could stop fooling himself. He'd lost his creative spark. The sooner he acknowledged that, the sooner he could give his full attention to the management of the firm. Let Larry handle the designs; he would work where he belonged, at the practical end of things.

Still, he felt a vague tug, as though he had lost a dear friend. To be expected, he rationalized. Maybe he should don black and have a proper funeral.

"That does it," Jackson said, jumping to his feet and toppling his chair. "Bargain? I'm losing money. If I'd gone with any other firm, we'd be in production by now. Instead, you two are still stuck to the drawing board like a pair of trapped flies."

John only half listened to the argument. Most of his attention was focused inside as he mourned his loss.

Dearly beloved, we're gathered here, not to praise, but to bury John's talents. The thought made him shudder, but the fact that it had entered his head in Wanda's voice startled him.

Listen Rocko, her voice continued, *you close the lid now, and you'll never get out of that box. Your creativity isn't dead, just confined in a straitjacket. Go ahead, pick up that pen. The world won't collapse if you draw a squiggly line.*

It resonated so clearly, he looked around expecting to see her in the room. Larry and Jackson were still the only others present.

"My grandmother would have a name for people like you," Larry said to Jackson.

"I'm sure it would be as colorful as your... costume," Jackson said, pointing to Larry's clothes. "But I'm not at all interested. Why I ever thought I could communicate with a dressed up Maypole, and Mr. Ho-hum over there, is beyond me. I'm through trying."

Jackson stormed toward the exit, but before he got there, the door banged open, and in floated a bouquet of balloons held by a woman in pink tights and a tutu.

"Are you John Rockman?" the pink lady asked an openmouthed Jackson. He shook his head, slow motion, and pointed across the room.

Smiling, she handed Jackson the balloons, then blew a whistle and cartwheeled into the room. She landed in a split in front of John.

"Happy thirty-fifth. May the year be full of surprises," she said, beaming broadly enough to crack her stage makeup.

"Let me out of here." Jackson turned toward the door, but found his escape blocked.

In walked a circus. Clowns, dancers, jugglers all pushed forward, carrying Jackson with them. John heard his client's screams of protest but couldn't help, since three confetti-throwing women had him trapped, also.

"Wanda," John whispered, then he shook his head innocently and pointed the dancers toward Larry. With the women gone, he looked down at his work and remembered the suggestions Wanda had made that afternoon in his hotel. The more he considered them, the more he realized their merit.

Excitement and surprise didn't have to mean disaster. An unexpected angle here, a sudden curve there would not destroy the design's integrity.

He grabbed a last look at the office chaos, at Larry pleasantly trapped by the dancing confetti sisters, at Jackson caught between two knife-wielding jugglers, and blocked it all out. An inner voice started directing his hand across the paper.

When he looked up again, he discovered Larry transformed into a papier-mâché *chotchkah,* and Jackson, red-faced with anger, hiding in a corner while the circus spilled out the door singing "Happy Birthday."

16

SILENCE REPLACED the singing. The three men eyed each other; not one of them moved. Suddenly a balloon popped, and the noise startled them into animation. They all spoke at once, Larry waving his arms and squeaking, Jackson shaking his finger and blasting like a trumpet.

John placed two fingers in his mouth and whistled.

"Quiet!" he shouted.

Silence.

"Mr. Jackson," he began.

"Mr. Jackson, nothing. No wonder you people can't come up with a decent design—you're too busy operating a carnival. Architecture must be your sideline, something to make you look normal. Well, I'm not fooled, and I'm not staying."

"Mr. Jackson." John used his deepest voice. His client froze with his hand stretched toward the doorknob. "You didn't witness a carnival, you experienced a tornado. I'm lucky it arrived in time to wake me up."

Jackson turned around, a puzzled look adding more angles to his face.

"A compromise," John said, holding up the changes he'd made. "Simplicity neither too stiff nor too shocking."

"I'm not interested," Jackson said, but his gaze locked onto the drawings.

"Don't leave without looking. If you don't like them, fine. We'll hang these with the others and use them for dart practice. Our relationship will be terminated."

Jackson snorted, but took the papers and spread them on the table. His face twisted into a snarl. He looked like a buzzard about to reject an offering of roadkill.

John's heart hit his chest as hard as a sledgehammer. Deep breathing didn't seem to calm it any. He had hoped to see a glimmer of satisfaction break through on his client's face, but Jackson's sour expression looked no different than it did at any other time.

Watching became impossible.

John noticed ink on his hands, grabbed a paper towel from his desk and began wiping. Soap and water would have served better, but he dared not leave the room. When he finished, he crumpled the paper, tossed it into the wastebasket and looked over at Jackson.

"Well?" he asked.

Jackson looked up, eyes sparkling.

"These are wonderful—perfect," he said. "Resembles your earlier work, only better." He returned to the drawings, smiling and shaking his head. "Why didn't you deliver sooner?"

"I had to travel to the eye of the storm first," John said.

WANDA LET THE RECEIVER fall back into place. She sat frozen, seeing only a blur. Her heart thumped so violently, vibrations lodged in her throat. From some distant tunnel, a chastising whisper blew an icy breath down her spine.

Fool.

What had John's receptionist said? That nothing had arrived for him. That he was in conference with a client until three-thirty.

What possessed her to send a birthday greeting to his office? She should have foreseen the problems. Having a group of circus clowns interrupt an important meeting qualified as the worst of all possible problems.

Thank goodness she'd called to check. At least now, she could rush to his office and hopefully arrive before the "greeting" did. But what if she was too late?

In a matter of minutes, Wanda was in her car and pulling out of her parking spot.

The dashboard clock displayed the hour in neon boldness. Two-forty-two. She'd told the performers anytime between two-thirty and three. John's office was a good twenty minutes away. If traffic on Connecticut Avenue proved lighter than usual and she drove like an aggressive cabbie, she just might make it.

She turned onto the street and maneuvered around two slower vehicles. Up ahead, the traffic moved at a steady pace—no snarls, no sightseers, no snails. She pushed harder on the gas pedal. Just then, a bus pulled away from the curb and stopped.

Wanda slammed on the brakes. Her car screeched to a stop. She pitched forward, then rammed back into her seat. Her fingers, white-knuckled, locked on the steering wheel. She loosened her grip and released her breath.

A few more inches and her front seat would be sitting in the back seat of the bus. Lucky, she thought, but changed her mind when she noticed the bus wasn't moving. Instead, its front doors opened and the driver waved across the street to a package-laden woman standing at the corner.

No, he wouldn't hold up traffic waiting for her? Wanda watched the lights change, watched the woman saunter across the street and watched the neon clock count down the minutes.

WHEN LARRY BOUNCED into his office, John didn't bother swiveling his chair around.

"Old Jackson was certainly happy, ready to hand out cigars, no less," Larry said and sat on the edge of the desk. "But you didn't have to play it so close. Zero-hour rescues do nothing for my nerves, man."

"It wasn't planned...far from it." John rested his chin atop his steepled fingertips. He gazed out the window at nothing in particular.

"The balloons, the dancers? Come on, the way Jackson got pinned between those jugglers...you didn't plan that?"

"Wanda."

Larry gave a short laugh. "That was better than her furniture trick."

Much better, though the message read the same— wake up and live. It took a circus to open his eyes. Thanks to Wanda, he would never let his own unyielding logic paralyze him again. Quite a birthday gift.

And what had he given her? Divorce papers.

His chest tightened with the gripping pain of loss. Wanda. How could he have sacrificed his marriage for his misguided sense of security? How could he have lost sight of what mattered most to him? Now, thanks to his stubbornness, he had lost her. The knot in his chest twisted tighter.

He had lost Wanda. The fact punched him in the stomach like a heavyweight's blow. He felt his breath escape and the blood drain from his head. He wavered, dizzy and sick with loss.

"You don't look so good, man. Not like someone who's just landed a half million dollar contract."

"We landed it all right, but at what price?"

"A couple of ulcers...no more."

"Wrong," John said. He shot out of his chair, and reached the door in a flash. "Too much more, but I'll fix that if I'm not already too late."

"You're leaving? I thought we were going to celebrate?"

"Start without me."

"Where're you going?"

"Back to the epicenter, and if I'm lucky, she may still feel a rumble for me."

17

JOHN DROVE FASTER than he should. He knew it. He only wished he could go faster, but P Street was too narrow for that. Even driving over the speed limit, he wouldn't get to Wanda's office in less than fifteen minutes. If the police stopped him, he could add on a ticket and another ten minutes.

And who could say she'd even be at work? According to Dusty, Wanda practically lived at her office, but often visited clients throughout the city. She could be in a meeting across town, or having a late lunch with a male client. That thought frightened him. He stepped heavier on the accelerator.

He should have called first instead of rushing out the way he had. Poor planning, Rocko. What was worse, he hadn't even planned what he'd say when they met face-to-face. Perhaps she wouldn't even want to see him.

Dupont Circle came into view. During warm weather, crowds flocked around its large fountain. On this fall day, no water sluiced over the full basin, but no one seemed to care. Pedestrians and traffic still congested the area.

Most drivers viewed the circle as an obstacle course of stoplights and right-turn-only lanes. John was no exception, but once around it, he could sail up Connecticut like a breeze.

He waited to make his turn off P Street. A woman driving a small yellow convertible cut a sharp right onto his street. She resembled Wanda, except the woman's hair was pulled into a tight bun and she was dressed in conservative gray.

As he drove on, he looked in his rearview mirror. The yellow car blocked the mouth of P Street; cars were snarled behind it. The woman blinked her turn signal twice before swinging back into the Circle. Horns blasted in her wake.

It is Wanda! No one else would dare drive like that.

SHE THOUGHT she recognized the blue Honda, but the driver leaned forward on the steering wheel as though he were trying to push the car through the heavy traffic. John always drove sitting ramrod straight, his head on the neck rest, his hands placed precisely at ten and two. This man looked much too fired up, too wild to be John.

As she signaled her turn, the man in the Honda made a right off P and mingled with the traffic on Dupont Circle. In that second, when they were side by side, she glanced at the driver.

It is John! And he was fast making his way to the other side of the fountain.

Her brakes screamed when she applied them. Horns cried all around her. She didn't care. Catching that blue car was all that mattered.

She flicked her blinker, blasted her own horn and pulled back into the circle traffic. As she crossed over into the far left lane, she could hear tires screeching, but they were behind her. She focused on the blue car too far up ahead.

A voice came from out of nowhere.

"You ever watch the Indy 500, sweetheart?" the Hollywood moll asked.

"Sure, once…maybe twice," she answered, as husky as ever.

"They've got one goal and one goal only."

"I'm missing the point." Wanda tailgated a mini-van that crawled in front of her and blocked her view.

"They want to get from point A to B…fast. Ever hear of them asking permission? Winners aren't the Mother-may-I types."

"So, you're saying—"

"Punch it, sister."

"Yes, madam." She swung her car into the right lane, passed two cars and swerved back into the left before getting trapped in a right-turn-only spot.

"Like those moves?" she asked.

"Shocking," the moll answered.

THIS IS NOT WORKING. John gnawed on his bottom lip. He was speeding to catch up with her, and could tell she was doing the same thing. Slowing down would only create a jam. He had to come up with a scheme. At this rate, they'd be circling forever, unless…

John angled his car against the oncoming traffic and stopped. He threw the gearshift into park, removed the keys and jumped out. He hit the street running. A chorus of honks and expletives jeered him as he raced across the line of cars.

NOW WHAT? Traffic had stalled. Wanda sat in the snarled mess and traced the cause of the jam right up to the blue car parked crosswise to the road.

Oh, no! He's had an accident.

Her skin chilled and erupted with stinging prickles. The blood drained from her head. She thought she would faint, but managed to pulled herself out of her car. Her stomach churned, her legs wobbled and she steadied herself against the door.

He's hurt. He's dead.

In that instance, everything stopped. The noise of the street became a drone. She was sure her heart stopped, too; she couldn't feel it, couldn't hear it. She focused all her attention on John's car. Nothing moved.

Then she spied him racing toward the fountain. He skirted around cars, paying no attention to the danger. But she did. He'd get hit at any moment and go sailing up into the sky. She watched in horror, hands to her mouth holding back her scream...

One car broke through the congestion, picking up speed as it rounded traffic. *That fool will hit John.* She squeezed her eyes shut and shrieked.

Brakes screeched. A stuck horn blared its one shrill note. Wanda opened her eyes.

John was standing, but he must have been hit. Any minute now, he'd fall. Instead, he put his hand on the hood, pushed away and was off and running.

He moved with such reckless energy, people scurried out of his path. He dodged this way, zigzagged that, pushing through the crowd clustered near the fountain. She'd never seen John move with such prowess.

It was then she saw the group of nursery-school

children linked hand in hand. They stretched across his path and stopped him dead. She watched him run up and down the line of tots, looking for an opening. None. He froze for a moment, then dashed directly for the fountain.

In one flying leap, he splashed into the basin. Water sprayed into the air as he ran through. She watched him jump out and head for her side of the street. Her heart pounded in her throat.

He slipped around the cars, making his way to her. But time suspended and John floated. Wanda's breath caught in her throat. Her stomach tightened as she waited, frozen, pressed against her car door.

Then he stood facing her, his suit coat open and hanging off one shoulder, his chest expanding with each heaving breath. His white shirt, wet and sticking to his torso, hung out of his waistband like an old washrag. Beads of water dripped from his hair and dotted his glasses.

He was safe. He was soaked. And he was crazy.

"Surprise," he said. The sun reflected on his glasses, hiding the expression in his eyes.

"Surprise? You could have been killed," she yelled, pointing at the snarled traffic. Her voice screeched above the car horns.

"Not a chance. I'm on a mission."

"You're on something all right, but I suspect it's a controlled substance. You've stopped traffic all the way to Capitol Hill, and you're standing here grinning like a monkey. What's gotten into you?"

"Some sense…finally."

"Running through traffic like that is anything but sensible. It's…it's…"

"Rash?"

"Yes, rash, and—"

"Spontaneous."

She jerked at his answer. Her mouth gaped and she gazed into his flushed face. That's exactly what it was, spontaneous, and so unlike John. She cocked her head and regarded him.

"I was on my way to your office," he said. "I got your 'message' this afternoon, and decided to deliver mine in person."

He placed one hand on his hip, the other on the car. His arm brushed her side. He pressed forward, almost touching her. The air between them crackled.

"I...I can explain. You see, I thought if you and I talked, face-to-face... I mean, if we met, the two of us, you'd change your mind about...things."

Darn. Her mouth felt like it had been vacuumed dry. This was the most important speech she would ever make and suddenly she'd forgotten English. She swallowed grit down her rough throat and tried again.

"Another scheme. I know I promised, but... Look, if the clowns bothered you, I'm sorry. I'm sorry I broke my promise, I'm sorr—"

"Wanda. Shut up."

"What?"

A smile broke the grim look on his face, then broadened until he opened into a roaring laugh. Motorists lowered their windows and stared, but John didn't seem to notice. Never could she remember him acting like that in public.

"What are... I don't—"

She didn't finish the sentence. He grabbed her around the waist, hoisted her into the air and plopped her atop the hood of her car. When she tried to speak, he covered her mouth with his.

His kiss sucked her breath away. She opened her eyes wide, then let them flutter closed. His lips moved over hers, tenderly. She melted into it and kissed him back in kind.

Every inch of her, inside and out, blossomed with warmth. She wrapped her arms around his neck, drawing him against her. His body shivered in response.

Finally, he pulled away. She reeled. If not for his firm grip on her waist, she would have slid right off the hood.

"Is this some sort of scheme," she asked, "or just your way of wooing a girl?"

"Both."

"What's supposed to happen next?"

"Boy wins girl. They live happily ever after."

"You sure?"

"My girl, my scheme. Can't end any other way."

"There're some things this boy and girl have to get straight first."

"Like the dog?"

"For starters. The dog."

"As long as we get him from the pound. One with sad eyes and desperately looking for a home."

"And the baby?" She held her breath.

"Don't tell me they have those at the pound, too?"

"No, silly." She punched his arm with a half-folded hand. "Are we going to have a baby?"

"No...not in the middle of traffic."

This time she swung at him, but he caught her wrist and kissed her open palm.

"Are we?" she asked, feeling the tickles travel from her hand to her breast.

"Soon as we get home, we'll start working on it."

"May take a while to get out of here. Some impetuous nut abandoned his car in the middle of the road. Caused one heck of a traffic jam."

"Imagine that," he said, and swooped her up into another kiss.

LOVE & LAUGH

INTO NOVEMBER!

#31 GOING OVERBOARD
Vicki Lewis Thompson

Chance Jefferson was in over his head, stranded on a houseboat with a gorgeous pain in the neck like Andi Lombard. Neither of them knew how to steer the darn thing, and to make matters worse, Chance couldn't keep his hands off his irritating, but oh-so-sexy shipmate. If he fell for Andi, would he sink or swim?

#32 SANDRA AND THE SCOUNDREL
Jacqueline Diamond

Sandra Duval was *not* having a good day. First the mayor snubbed her at a charity fund-raiser! And then she was kidnapped! And swindled out of a fortune. The only way to save the day was to marry her kidnapper. Well, the man was gorgeous and even now Sandra believed you had to look for the silver lining....

Chuckles available now:

#29 ACCIDENTAL ROOMMATES
Charlotte Maclay
#30 WOOING WANDA
Gwen Pemberton

LOVE & LAUGHTER™

HARLEQUIN WOMEN KNOW ROMANCE WHEN THEY SEE IT.

And they'll see it on **ROMANCE CLASSICS**, the new 24-hour TV channel devoted to romantic movies and original programs like the special **Harlequin® Showcase of Authors & Stories.**

The **Harlequin® Showcase of Authors & Stories** introduces you to many of your favorite romance authors in a program developed exclusively for Harlequin® readers.

Watch for the **Harlequin® Showcase of Authors & Stories** series beginning in the summer of 1997.

If you're not receiving ROMANCE CLASSICS, call your local cable operator or satellite provider and ask for it today!

ROMANCE CLASSICS

Escape to the network of your dreams.

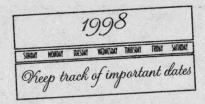

Three beautiful and colorful calendars that celebrate some of the most popular trends in America today.

Look for:

Just Babies—a 16 month calendar that features a full year of absolutely adorable babies!

1998 CALENDAR
Just Babies
16 months of adorable bundles of joy!

Hometown Quilts
1998 Calendar
A 16 month quilting extravaganza!

Hometown Quilts—a 16 month calendar featuring quilted art squares, plus a short history on twelve different quilt patterns.

Inspirations—a 16 month calendar with inspiring pictures and quotations.

Inspirations

A 16 month calendar that will lift your spirits and gladden your heart

Steeple Hill™

◇ HARLEQUIN®

Value priced at $9.99 U.S./$11.99 CAN., these calendars make a perfect gift!

Available in retail outlets in August 1997. CAL98

Coming in August 1997!

THE BETTY NEELS RUBY COLLECTION

August 1997—Stars Through the Mist
September 1997—The Doubtful Marriage
October 1997—The End of the Rainbow
November 1997—Three for a Wedding
December 1997—Roses for Christmas
January 1998—The Hasty Marriage

COLLECTOR'S EDITION

This August start assembling the
Betty Neels Ruby Collection. Six of the
most requested and best-loved titles have
been especially chosen for this collection.
From August 1997 until January 1998,
one title per month will be available to avid
fans. Spot the collection by the lush ruby red
cover with the gold Collector's Edition banner
and your favorite author's name—Betty Neels!

Available in August at your favorite retail outlet.

HARLEQUIN®

HARLEQUIN®

AMERICAN ◆ ROMANCE®
®

It's a stampede...to the altar!

WILD WEST
Weddings

by Cathy Gillen Thacker

You loved Montana maven Max McKendrick who gave his nephews and niece forty-eight hours to marry the spouses of his choice—in the first three Wild West Weddings books.

Now that wily ol' coot is back—and at the triple wedding ceremony he's given his family attorney, "Cisco" Kidd, an ultimatum: not only marry Ms. Gillian Taylor, but *stay* married to her for a week!

Don't miss the grand finale to the wacky, wonderful Wild West Weddings:

SPUR-OF-THE-MOMENT MARRIAGE (#697)

Available October 1997 wherever Harlequin books are sold.

The West was never this much fun!